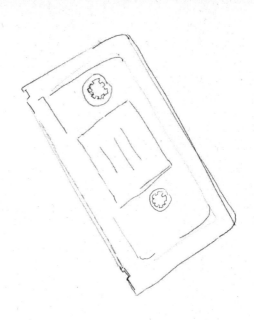

HERE IS WHERE

A novelette

MORGAN OMOTOYE

OPEN PEN

First Published in 2021
by Open Pen, 25 Crescent Road, London, E13 0LU

openpen.co.uk

9781838210618

OPNOV010

OPEN PEN NOVELETTES #8
"Here Is Where"
First Edition
© Morgan Omotoye 2021
Cover illustration by Pierre Buttin - pierrebuttin.com
© Pierre Buttin 2021

Stanza from "Self-Portrait on a Summer Evening" by Eavan Boland (© Eavan Boland 1987)

What you are watching
is light unlearning itself,
an infinite unlocking of the prism.
Eavan Boland

I answered the phone on its second ring. I knew it was her. It could only ever be her. Dorothy tended to call at night. I'd be hard-pressed to recall a single occasion when she rang during the day. Can't say I minded too tough. It made me feel special, as if I were a secret. Something she only braved uncover by the light of the silvery moon when her parents and younger brother, Stanley, were fast asleep. It was as though I were something cravingly precious, saved, squirrelled away during the chaotic, daylight hours only to be revealed and engaged with at the appropriate magical moment which tended to arrive between the hours of 12 and 3 in the a.m.

Whenever Dorothy rang it was usually to talk about someone she'd been out with. Could be some guy from 6th Form with too tight trousers or some flash, silver-tongued fella with accidental flair she met at a party while snarly music, heavy with intimidating 70s synch blasted out carefully sequestered speakers.

Years ago, Dorothy rang to speak about a date she'd been on with a magician named Tolliver, an acquaintance, I was to later learn, of Bootleg Traci's older brother, Stuyvesant Mifsud. Dorothy and Tolliver's date, if memory serves, took place in an Indian Restaurant called The Bengali Tiger, a stone's throw from Seven Sisters tube station.

I was sitting in bed with a pillow tightly pressed against my belly to ward off period pain which every time I was stupid enough to think I tamed, grew another pair of sharp, eager teeth, determined to gnaw away at my stomach lining, forcing me to squeeze and push my pillow into shapes which seemed part of an old ceremony demanding sacrifice and fire.

I don't mind saying I preferred the spinach green, star-shaped hot-water bottle as a palliative, but it had gone and sprung a leak, big time! Before the leak, gotta admit, the burnt rubber smell wafting up from the gaping nozzle whenever I poured scalding water down the hot-water bottle's throat made me queasy behind my eyes while the grubbily expectant way the counterfeit star swelled up, all satisfied and sure of itself like a tick gorging on blood put the wind up me something fierce. Throwing the star-shaped, spinach green hot-water bottle in the bin when I became aware of the leak (keeping in mind the other negatives going against it) was super easy. Well, OK, sure. I missed the kitchen bin by a country mile on my first attempt. Got it in on my second go. OK third, after Mum and Mastermind kept staring at me like I'd lost my marbles. OK fourth, after Mastermind trotted away to preserve what little remained of my dignity and Mum, God love her, held the grey kitchen bin lid open for me with a thoughtful look on her face. OK fifth.

While Dorothy spoke, I pictured her calmly coiling and uncoiling the lengthy white telephone flex cord around and around her middle finger. I closed my eyes to fully savour the image, its languid insolence reminiscent of a steamed foot, sinking into obscurity beneath lavender scented, bathwater. I sighed deeply into the crumpled top half of my pillow before snapping my eyes wide open. I was worried Dorothy heard me. She hadn't. She was still speaking.

She said the tall white balustrades on either side of the

restaurant entrance were imposing like municipal buildings from the 1930s. She described the inside of the restaurant as fussily long, like a giraffe's neck.

She said the tables were circular and disastrously small. Point of fact she likened them to poor man's descendants of King Arthur's Round Table and they were all, down to the very last, draped under pink tablecloths with absolutely no patterns on them, not a trace. The tablecloths were as pink as Mastermind's tongue Dorothy added with a throaty laugh that came close to making me lose my grip on my pillow. To prevent my pillow from reaching the floor and toppling the pile of books near my bed I had to clench it firmly between my thighs. Even though I had my pillow I was really starting to miss the spinach green, star-shaped, hot-water bottle, especially its warmth, guaranteed by its packaging to last for up to six hours.

Dorothy was still speaking. She said The Bengali Tiger was jammed with patrons talking loudly and waving their hands about to draw more attention to their words. It was difficult then annoying then difficult all over again trying to hear what Tolliver said. Despite this Dorothy swore blind she enjoyed the rather focused and intense way Tolliver stared into her eyes like he was determined to hypnotise her into letting him pull her pants off. Dorothy had no doubt her pants were staying on. Her pants, far as I knew, always stayed on.

There were times Dorothy found herself laughing at Tolliver's jokes whenever she managed to catch or intuit their punchlines above the booming voices rising in unison every now and then from other tables. I took Dorothy at her word, although I suspected, at some point, I was going to have to ask her to repeat one of Tolliver's jokes because nothing she'd said about him left me with the impression he had a funny bone located anywhere on his body.

Not once did Dorothy take the time to mention Tolliver's hands; you'd think she would. Him being a magician and all. A profession in which sleights of hand and other devilment with hands were of singular and marked importance. Nope. Nah-dah. Not once did Dorothy utter a single word about Tolliver's hands, although I kept expecting her to. I kept waiting to hear her declare heartily, 'Pacific, you should have seen his hands.' The fact these words never appeared left me with a dull ache of anticipation hunkered beneath my rib cage I thought pressing my pillow deeper into my belly would alleviate. It didn't.

Eventually, Dorothy got round to speaking about the paintings on the walls. The Bengali Tiger was full of them. Even the tooth-achingly bright toilet with its tawdry spool of bog roll had paintings hanging on the walls and the back of the toilet door, which was something Dorothy had never seen before and figured she would never see again.

Every single painting depicted the same scene a number of artists had been commissioned to reproduce in various styles. Ranging from egg tempera on canvas, acrylic on board, compressed charcoal on torn paper, and one particularly mysterious one floating above the cash register, composed, it seemed, entirely of smoke.

Every painting revealed fecund jungle scapes with barrel-chested men decked in camouflage. The men owned handlebar moustaches like industrious Victorian types going about their mid-afternoon perambulations and if not that exactly then certainly their modern-day equivalents, Hoxton so-and-sos on the pull. There were flashing sabres and scimitars attached to their bulging hips. Some of the men had fancy epaulets of arcane or possibly heraldic design gleaming resplendently from their shoulders like sunlight glancing off the brim of a conquistador's morion helmet. All the men carried guns. Incredibly antiquated firearms, on the verge of breaking apart, lending them a curious air of vulnerability like an overspill car park with one car in it, then no car.

The men in the paintings were hunting. Busy with the dangerous work of stalking tigers. In every painting a tiger. Sometimes fat and swollen as a balloon filled with water, other times lithe and willowy as a single blade of grass. The tigers were always fleeing the scene. Making for the shadowed recesses of the jungle.

'That's all kind of strange,' I cooed a little too excitedly. 'Why would a place called The Bengali Tiger have paintings in which tigers were being hunted? You'd think it'd be, I dunno, the exact opposite. Like maybe they'd be revered or something. Worshipped even.'

'I suppose,' Dorothy said absently.

'So why do you think they're there in the first place?'

'Say again,' Dorothy said.

'The paintings, why do you think they're there?'

'Fuck I know?' Dorothy said.

Just like she hadn't spoken about Tolliver's hands; how slowly his fingers traced the filigree brocade of the dessert spoon handle or carefully whisked a sparkling pound coin from behind her head, not once did Dorothy mention food. A sure-fire sign the food wasn't all that.

I remember thinking Tolliver's name made him sound tall like Lurch from *The Addams Family*. I was this close, hand on heart; if I'm lying I'm dying, to asking Dorothy if Tolliver was tall like Lurch from *The Addams Family* and if this affected the pattern of his kisses. How they might have plummeted from his lips with the sombre motion of a rabbit or possibly a dove, being stuffed inside a magician's felt top hat or did she end up having to do all the work? Her neck strings bulging with effort as she stood on tiptoes to meet his mouth? With this line of inquiry fizzing away like electrified sugar on the tip of my tongue I zigged when I should have zagged.

I asked if Tolliver made himself disappear when the bill arrived.

I laughed after saying this, my whole body shaking with the bright surprise of my words which kept detonating in front of me, like-like-like when a magician keeps pulling an inexhaustible stream of linked, multicoloured handkerchiefs from inside their right sleeve. I also felt a bolt of energy shoot down my legs which I took to be a close enough approximation to the wondrous glee the Gingerbread Man must have felt in his first giddy moments of sentience. Before every single thing: in front, behind, to his left, his right, above and below, revealed he had to hit the road at a run.

I could also picture with great acuity, forensic in its scope, the puff of smoke materialising to take Tolliver's place the second he disappeared. I saw Dorothy too. Quite sensibly, quite understandably, staring into absence, into void. I saw the stricken look of surprise take hold of her rigorously triangular-shaped face as her stubby fingers skirted over the tablecloth. Seeking abrasions and inversions on the soft pink fabric she could distract herself with.

I began to wonder, what if the magician's greatest trick, was not to vanish so completely but to actually, transform into me. Say in the blink of an eye it was me, yours truly, sitting opposite Dorothy in The Bengali Tiger. Me ignoring the legion of frightfully odd paintings on the walls. Me witnessing the succulent 'O' of Dorothy's mouth as she gawped away in amazement at my sudden appearance.

I should add for prosperity as my laughter raspily winded down I was already losing myself to the supple intimacies of Dorothy's mouth. I couldn't help wondering what her lips would taste of as we kissed. Spicy lamb bhuna with trace amounts of a fluffy mint sauce or maybe tangy apple from apple juice concentrate two days shy of its expiration date. Too bad, too sad, Dorothy hadn't mentioned food or drink so there was more than a good chance she wouldn't taste of anything.

Let's just say for argument's sake I wasn't on the telephone with Dorothy or imagining sitting opposite her in The Bengali Tiger but I dunno abracadabra alakazam, I was suddenly with her in her bedroom with its squad of soft toys bivouacked on the long plywood shelf floating above her bed. Say I was there.

Me. Sitting on her bed, paying little to no attention to the probing gaze of pop stars, from the posters on her wall. Me. Under the tender bellies of the soft toys on her shelf: lions, tigers, teddy bears, rabbits, elephants, and a plush cephalopod true to life with all the coiled tentacles of the real thing but owning a heart-shaped mouth and it was me. Kissing Dorothy and being kissed by her. Over and over and over and over.

Dorothy slammed the phone down!

This had never happened before. Usually, I just listened to Dorothy talk; offering sympathetic ums and ahhhs at crucial junctures. This time round – I don't know why exactly – I made a stupid joke and Dorothy, who could and often did stay on the phone for hours, put the finishing end to our conversation in such an abrupt and decisive manner I believed she was joking. Had to be. She'd ring back soon. Of course she would. Her voice scoured free of flavour like a show kitchen and as a peace offering, to nudge her further from her strop I would promise, no joke, to give, not lend, straight up give her my favourite issue of *Smash Hits* with the amazing Neneh Cherry on the cover.

I knew Dorothy coveted this issue like no other because it had an interview with Chesney Hawkes (Yammering on about his film *Buddy's Song*.) and a double-sided poster of T'Pau looking more T'Pauish than ever. The peace deal brokered, Dorothy and I would talk away any awkwardness between us with me promising to watch my mouth and Dorothy agreeing to keep me company while I played the arcade game *Midnight Resistance* even though she wasn't at all enamoured with the dingy, sour-smelling video shop in which the arcade machine was housed. As we spoke, we would gradually get round to drawing up plans to meet up after school the next day at Trolley Park, where we rammed abandoned shopping trolleys from competing supermarket chains into each other.

Dorothy sticking with the theory shopping trolleys from Nettos were a hundred times more durable than any other shopping trolley due to their dignified, Terrier dog masthead, and me absolutely loyal to Kwik Save trolleys on account of the fact I admired the pneumatic heft of their wheels and the gurgly sucking sound they made over the gravelled ground.

Trolley Park wasn't really a park-park, with your archetypical deciduous trees, everyday quack-quaking ducks, or gloomy park benches patiently waiting to be put out of their misery. It was the back of a council estate garage near my school Dorothy and I chanced upon, on one of our long walks when we were first getting to know each other.

The second we caught sight of the shopping trolleys, forlorn and unceremoniously dumped in front of the garage wall we knew exactly what needed to happen to them. Like jousting knights of yore, Dorothy and I charged at each other with our chosen shopping trolley grasped firmly in front of us. The object of the game was to see who would swerve out of the way before sense shattering, impact. Neither of us ever did, which means the cost of losing remains as elusive to me now as it did back then.

More often than not, we'd get told off. Alerted by the grinding, metallic screech of shopping trolleys colliding, entwined with whooping war cries, released at the top of our lungs, someone, rudimentarily fleshed out in the autobiography of the living room, the vegetal heat of the living room sofa, the powdery blue light of a TV show, would push open their living room window with blatantly more force than was absolutely necessary. Their face, humming with the pugnacious scowl made infamous by Nora Batty from *Last of the Summer Wine*, they waved angrily at us, before threatening to call the police. Sufficiently panicked, this was my cue to hit the bricks with a meek sad sack droop of my shoulders and mumbled words of apology but Dorothy; standing tall, placed her hands over her ears and slowly pulled her hands away from her ears. She carefully rotated both hands forward and back in tiny –blink and you'd miss them–half-circles, indicating she couldn't hear but was doing her best to tune into what was being said. Not so much said, as hollered.

From where I stood, it looked like Dorothy was placing an invisible pair of bulky headphones over her head and adjusting the padded cushions for maximum comfort. Witnessing this convinced me to continue working on the compilation tape I was making her. Side A was pretty much done and dusted. Side B was nowhere near complete.

In next to no time I'd hear the living room window slam shut, with blatantly more force than was necessary. As for the local constabulary, they never appeared, which must stand as a miracle for the ages.

I was certain Dorothy would ring back. Any minute now. Waiting to hear from her I laid down on my bed and thought about the two of us, exhausted by our efforts, collapsing on the ground riddled with bottle tops, rubber bands flaunting their flexibility by retaining shapes that would make a Möbius strip blush and question its career choice. Flattened Five Alive juice boxes missing their give-away, holographic *Sharky and George* stickers, a keyring with a set of keys corrupted by rust and the decapitated head from a Mumm-Ra the Ever-Living action figure, with one of the two snakes adorning his headpiece chewed to a messy clump. Dorothy and I calmly lay amongst these things. The palms of our hands stinging like we'd been bitten by about a million ants due to the juddering, jouncing impact of the shopping trolleys we smashed into each other with more kinetic energy than seemed possible for two girls to generate at such short notice and true-say, without much of a run-up. Dorothy and I, catching our breath, look up.

Past the roofs of garages happy and content being garage roofs for always. Past football flags dangling from balcony irons like battle standards. Past the chimney of the nearby launderette emitting puffs of steam as thick and white as the spume in Hokusai's famed drawing *The Great Wave off Kanagawa*.

'I can see these fuzzy, squiggly dots dancing in front of my eyes,' Dorothy said, as a ladybug heading home from a reconnaissance mission hung above her head. Making up its mind whether or not to land in her hair.

'I don't see them,' I said.

'They're beautiful,' Dorothy said, her voice fragile, with unadulterated delight. Her hands were reaching up, trying to corral what she saw into my line of sight. 'Can't you see them?' Dorothy asked as the ladybird, deciding it was best to stay out of human affairs, flew homeward.

'No,' I said, trying not to sound irritated by the fact Dorothy and I were looking at the same sky and seeing different things.

Dorothy does not ring back.

Three weeks go by.

I moped and sulked around the house like a ghost haunting the furniture of the people who would live in our house a hundred years from now. Mum kept placing her right hand on my forehead to check if I had a temperature. Fact I didn't, mystified us.

'What's going on here then?' Mum asked, gazing at her right hand as though it were faulty.

'Beats me,' I replied.

I could have phoned Dorothy. I had a feeling though, a niggling suspicion this would be the wrong thing to do. From the get-go, Dorothy always rang me. I was always the one waiting for her to call. Such a resolute pattern of behaviour, of call and response, could not be changed or otherwise tampered with.

Four months go by.

During this time food tasted like it was wrapped in cellophane and when it didn't taste like it was wrapped in cellophane, it tasted burped up, as if the crucial work of mastication had been achieved by a stand-in while I was elsewhere, possibly watching cartoons with tear-stained eyes or in my bedroom trying to stare past the ceiling into the wealth of sky I knew existed but had worlds of trouble believing in.

Mum, after failing to rouse my spirits by getting me to watch my favourite film, *Adventures in Babysitting* with actress extraordinaire Elisabeth Shue, would knock on my bedroom door, quiet and respectful like I was a shell-shocked convalescent earmarked for a chairlift and a 2000 piece jigsaw puzzle depicting heart-warming scenes from before The Crimean War. Mum, doing her best to help, rented a video cassette from Moonlight Video and left it for me on the kitchen table. I don't watch the video. I leave it on the kitchen table. When Mum took the video cassette back, the late fees made her blink. Mum, sitting at the foot of my bed and tenderly messaging my feet, would talk to me. Telling me about my name, the saga, and rumour of its origins. She would talk me a future, one in which I was incandescently happy, bursting with the sort of inner light too bright to look at for very long. She would speak to me for hours as I grew increasingly annoyed with her because I knew she had to get up early for work. There was also a quality to her vigilance, close to hysteria which made me wary of her. Mum was eagle-eyed, watching for any sign of change. In how I spoke, moved, or failed to move. She was also looking for tell-tale signs she'd missed with Dad. I had a sense of her being obscurely prepared, as though my predicament was written down in a book of tasks mothers prepare for, and to some extent looked forward to. Mum, after taking tiny sips from a mug filled with sassafras tea, would ask, if I was I sure I didn't want a warm cup of Milo to help me sleep. I knew before she gave it to me to drink, Mum would blow on it.

In Dorothy's absence, I stopped listening to music. Which meant I stopped working on the compilation tape I was making her. There was room left for at least one more song on Side B, at a push. Once this song was added I hoped, fingers crossed, I'd be able to come up with a title for the compilation tape. This was proving just as difficult as settling on what the last song had to be. The last song needed to be a culmination of all the songs that had gone before but also be nothing at all like any of the songs that had gone before, if that makes a lick of sense. I rattled my brains to grated cheese trying to figure out what this song could be, had to be. I sought Mastermind's counsel but he wasn't much use. I raided and ransacked Mum's records and wasn't very careful putting them back in the cupboard. This, I'm sure, combined with the fact I'd forgotten to put money on the electricity key made Mum annoyed with me. When I asked Mum for recommendations and she suggested Michael Bolton, I knew, for sure, Mum had gone beyond being annoyed and was pissed.

I began sleeping with the unfinished compilation tape under my pillow, in vain hope, any inspiration revealing itself in my dreams would seep into it.

When I didn't hear from Dorothy I couldn't wait to get rid of the tape. It was embarrassing, the length of hours I spent waiting for songs to come on the radio, cueing up songs on the Sanyo double-deck tape player in the front room. The longer I didn't hear from Dorothy the more I thought about chucking the cassette in the River Lea. I go one step further than just thinking about it. Early one morning, before school, the tape was in my hand, and in my mind, I heard the splash it would make as it slowly sunk beneath the algae scabbed waters of the River Lea. I saw the ripples it would form waylay a journeying water boatman. Hand on heart, I lifted the tape to throw and be rid of for always when a lone cormorant, perched on a half-submerged log, seized me up. The cormorant stared at me. I stared at the cormorant. The cormorant stared at me. I stared at the cormorant. There was mist on the water. Yellow butterflies rising from ling heather brailed the atmosphere with everything they failed to say when they were caterpillars. A flotilla of frog spawn clung to the water's edge. The cormorant looked away when I carefully returned the tape to my pocket.

In Dorothy's absence I also stopped reading, no, that's not true exactly. Mm, I mean, I still read but I could only focus on the books I devoured as a child. Stories by Babette Cole and Ladybird Fairytales. After a while Babette Cole's lissom drawings failed to elicit any response from me and try as I might I couldn't get past the first four pages of the Ladybird version of *Rapunzel*. I got no further than the scene where Rapunzel lets down her hair for the Prince to clamber up. I put the books back on the shelf. They stared at me accusingly like I'd abandoned them to an era of broken hearts. I stuffed them in a bin liner bulging with old clothes and carted the lot down to Oxfam on the high street. Oxfam was closed, so I carted the whole kit and caboodle to Age Concern. I thought about putting the tape in the bag but the memory of the cormorant's unwavering gaze stayed my hand.

I still played arcade machines. I mean, I played *Midnight Resistance* until it was replaced by a game with a massive machine gun for a joystick. When you used the machine gun on characters in the game, pixelated blood and brain juice, the dowdy colour of chewed to death chewing gum, spurted from their heads. You lost points when you shot hostages. On more than one occasion I went kill-crazy and mowed down everything in sight, with no thought given to the fact my ammo was running low and I was reducing my chances of achieving a high score. I didn't enjoy playing this game too tough and decided to allow arcade games for a bit.

Meanwhile, Mastermind, our black cat, with paws which looked like he'd stepped in a roller tray filled with white paint began observing me with glints of worry coalescing in his eyes of amber-green but I don't know? Whenever I closed my bedroom door to keep him with me, he scratched and clawed away at it with furious abandon. When I eventually got round to opening the door, Mastermind darted down the stairs like he was being stalked and hunted, like he somehow knew, through some form of cat Juju of all the lurid paintings hanging in The Bengali Tiger and was doing his utmost best to avoid the fate of his distant relatives. I felt betrayed by his departure and started avoiding him. For a while there, Mastermind avoided me, spending his nights on streets filled with starving cats.

During all this, I sometimes wandered over to Down Hills

Park, a few streets from my house. How you got there was make your way down my street like it was any other street, take a right, then another right bringing you up to Langham School (a moribund cluster of grey buildings) to your left and you're there. Ta-dah, Down Hills Park.

Say for me I usually sat on wooden park benches the colour of old pencil shavings and stared. I stared at Rugby posts emerging from the earth like the bones of some prehistoric beastie or, I suppose, a ladder, missing the necessary rungs, anti-slip safety feet, and slide rail enabling it to be a viable scaffold to another world. I stared at trees rampant with luscious green leaves because it was the ridiculous height of summer. Fact I felt, how can I say? Out of sorts, seemed to make the sun shine brighter, which I tried not to take personally, although to be fair, sometimes all you really want to do is punch the sun in its chin. After staring at trees and being suitably transfixed by rustling leaves caught in a sudden blush of silver due to their undersides casually exposed by a passing breeze, I stared at the sky. Relieved to discover it still existed.

The sky was scintillating blue and perfect. I really wanted to appreciate its beauty more. I couldn't. I kept encountering my hurt and bewilderment like a piece of bone stuck in my throat. The more I stared at the sky the more fidgety and desperate I grew to find within it a sort of manic freedom which would enable me to leave the present moment behind. This battlefield of time I was struggling to get through. I wanted to dissolve into the sky's blue immensity and become the me of aftermath already. I would be a heroine, remote, born of fire.

Wizened and grizzled with knowledge gained from hard-won experience. Scrappy with scars telling the story of where I'd been and in some cases where I was going.

The sky was yes-yes-yes, I believe I mentioned this already, astoundingly beautiful. Truly a jackpot of a sky. It was also as far away as sky can be so I stopped staring at it like it owed me money and focused my attention on joggers rushing past. Some of them glanced at me, with an almost imperceptible shaking of their heads, as though there was a small pebble lodged in their auditory canal, they were determined to shake loose without seeming to have to try. I was surprised to find myself envious of their omnivorous energy, the perky eagerness of their muscles working in frictionless tandem like darkness and starlight. I hate to admit it, but I was somewhat flabbergasted by the insatiable confidence these joggers projected, giving them the ability to display themselves in front of everyone and everything that might be watching, without it seemed to me, a single care in the world.

I knew if I stayed longer, I'd mumble something nonsensical in their general direction like, 'Fatty be food and follow me.' If not that, there was a good chance I'd end up asking for directions to the very park I sat in.

'You're here,' the jogger would reply.

I decided to keep my mouth shut. Besides I really didn't want to hear my voice brushing over the landscape of another human being, the irregular creases on their sweat sodden shirt, the mulch of nutrient-rich dirt caked under their fingernails so I headed home, quick smart. Back to my bedroom. Mum's surveillance, Mastermind's absence. The unassailable fact of the ceiling.

Make no mistake, there was school. Mum, God love her, made sure I went. Every second there felt like everyone, from Bootleg Traci, teachers, relief teachers, classmates, dinner ladies, Shrapnel Face Mike the school caretaker, danced around my bones.

Oh yeah, silly me, I nearly forgot to mention all of this took place during the season when for some peculiar reason whenever I stood in front of sliding doors, they refused to slide open for me. Whatever sensors or thingamajigs gauging my presence, on the fritz, big timers. Strangely enough, this was also around the time I was forever and a day setting off alarms in shops. Even when I didn't have anything from the shops on my person, the alarms would shriek like a pig perforated with a pointy stick. I raised my hands high above my head as security guards emerged from the shadows, their walkie-talkies hiccupping wild burrs of static. The security guards approached me cautiously like they weren't quite sure what to expect from someone so eager to assume blame.

I was stranded with no sense of belonging in my skin and my poor mum, tried her best to help me. Coming into my room late at night, quiet as a haunt, and sitting with me, changing tact now and speaking of her bad breed, brought up by her bootstraps life. Mum. Showing me the jagged scar on her left knee. Telling me the wonder tale of how she acquired it. Mum. Speaking about the time she caught a lift to the main road in an open-backed truck. Shiko, the family dog, a large

German shepherd, spying on her from the eastern side of the house. Shiko had never seen this truck before, in all the days and nights he drew breath in Jamaica he had never laid eyes on this truck. He did not know the people in this truck. Shiko saw my mother jumping in the back of the truck. Shiko chased the truck down. My mother, Mum, bemused by his barking and the gregarious amount of slobber flying from his mouth, continued screaming his name as the truck picked up speed.

Hours later, walking home and hugging close to her chest a brand-new Oxblood satchel with more buckles and straps than she knew what to do with. My mother, thinking thoughts about the genips in her pockets and the shiny metal pencil case in her satchel. My mum, just having thoughts. Whistling at one point, then not, pirouetting at one point, then not. Mum. Her hair a maelstrom of clip-on barrettes, a number of which were moulded and shaped into fruit not indigenous to the country she was born in. Closer to home Mum saw Shiko's bloody paw prints on the pebbly road. She broke into a run with tears in her eyes.

Mum spoke. I listened. She was offering me her patience, her understanding, her love. She was sitting right next to me but I felt closer to Dad. Closer than I ever felt picking my way through his books. Closer than I ever felt amongst the tools of his trade, his hammers, power saws and screwdrivers. His spiral-bound notebooks filled with measurements for joists and beams and other jotted marginalia Mum let me study for a while, then took away.

I listened, feeling detached from Mum and closer to

Dad, convinced I glimpsed something peaceable in his final moments. Mum found him. She scraped his dried blood off the tracking buttons on the video cassette player with her fingernails before using a brillo pad. Mum carried the video player from our old house and dumped it in a skip. Mum. Went to the police station to retrieve a jiffy bag filled with all the things Dad had in his pockets. It was Mum and I standing in the back garden watching sparks curl up from the brillo pad Mum set on fire. Mum and I shivering in the full-on dark as I took a deep breath through my nose because I wanted to know what burning blood smelled like.

Mum was talking. She was sitting right next to me. And yet it was as though there was a fine mesh of mosquito netting between us. Through it I could fully discern the outline of my mother. Mum could reach out and touch me if she wanted. I could reach out and touch her. This vision, replete with intimacy, positively filthy with it, held no promise of communication. You'd be forgiven for thinking the soft transparency of the material separating us suggested the exact opposite since a single movement, a breath, was more than enough to dispel its parameters and bring us closer. It wasn't. I was a closed system and Heaven help me I was glad.

Our telephone was cordless. Its blunt square face had an LED display, the golden-brown of a decayed tooth. After Mum stopped speaking and finally left my room, I would hold the phone close to my face and begin pressing random buttons in the dark. The LED display lit up. I honestly can't say how much time was lost to me touching buttons just to see and be close to this quadrant of light.

I fell asleep. I called it sleep, although it was more like being wedged inside a cod liver oil capsule. I often woke bedraggled as though the cod liver oil capsule I was trapped in had been swallowed by an Anaconda with a serious case of hiccups.

With everything I've just told you, it should come as no surprise I could not focus on my studies. My A-level exams were looming around the corner. I couldn't afford to slack off, not one tinny, little bit, but I did.

I forced myself to read and engage with Schopenhauer's nihilistic exhortations so doom-laden to become hilarious and if it wasn't Schopenhauer waxing lyrical about music being the highest form of art then it was Shelly's epic poem, 'Queen Mab', harping on about, "Death, and his brother Sleep!" or some long-off, going round the houses chapter about 'Family,' in my Sociology *Haralambos and Holborn* textbook, I had to grabble with. The words in these texts wouldn't stay in place. They kept turning into ants scurrying off the page because they heard the ladybug's house was on fire and they were duty-bound to feed their bodies to the conflagration.

As days listlessly coalesced into weeks, a month, two months, three, I found myself, standing in front of Dorothy's house. I did not knock on her door. I stood on the opposite side of the road, hoping to be seen, dreading being seen. Standing in front of Dorothy's house and absolutely not knocking on her door became something along the lines of an endurance test, like imbibing poison to build up a tolerance. I believed, standing there I was growing stronger, divesting myself of my craving for her.

It was during one of these excursions I glimpsed Dorothy behind a Chloe gauze curtain. I watched her hand lift something from a table, although, hold the phone, Stanley's bedroom faced the street, so maybe it was Stanley's hand in motion I caught sight of as a dusty white van went hurtling past with Ray Charles booming from over-amped speakers. My eyes tracked the van, its undulating trail of music. When I looked back at the window, the shape was gone.

I don't easily recall how I left. Chances are I stumbled away, unable to meet the eyes of strangers walking past, petrified I was in love with them too. I saw right into them. I knew all about them, more than I possibly should. This fair-haired wonder by the peeling post-box, struggling with her yellow suitcase due to a dodgy back wheel. This man bending low to explain something to his daughter, her tiny face puffy with tears. I knew the scuffed miracle of their lives and as I moved among them I felt my heart sickeningly expand, grow monstrous and leaky with love, love, love, spilling out of me like water from the rip in the spinach green, star-shaped hot-water bottle I threw away.

I met Dorothy nine months prior to the events I'm telling you about. I accidentally padlock my bicycle to her bicycle. I was running super late and wanted to make sure I got a study carrel near the windows and not one close to the main counter. Where if I was unfortunate to wind up sitting, meant getting distracted by librarians cackling about the sexual peccadilloes of their line managers while patrons boisterously asked after novelisations of shows they'd watched on TV like *Mr. Majeika*,

Man in a Suitcase, or *The Terrible Shmoo*. In my haste to get to a quiet seat, I placed my D-lock over the bike stand closest to the library entrance and the top tube of Dorothy's bicycle.

When Dorothy saw her bicycle padlocked to mine, she told me she said, 'What next-level bullshit is this?'

She raged through cafés searching for the culprit, causing one bearded trendy type to drop his avocado sandwich into his Flat White. Heroically gauging the banshee aggro look in Dorothy's eyes he knew to continue sipping away as though his life depended on it. With the speed of an imp unleashed from Hell's darkest chamber, Dorothy made her way through the nearby sweet shops, knocking Jaffa cakes, Wagon Wheels, and packets of Canderel from their moorings. She blazed through fish and chips shops, kebab shops, a bookmaker (the *Hackney Gazette* would later reveal as a hideout for villains), and Argos, where she skilfully pocketed one of those minuscule blue pens used to fill in order forms. When she eventually set her sights on the library, her hair was all berserk about her face in a fiendishly elemental way like the hair of a witch perched over a bubbling cauldron bursting with eye of newt, frowzy torso of bat, and other diabolical accruements too terrible to mention here.

Dorothy hollered a slight variation of what she shouted in all the other places she rampaged through, with one crucial difference, expletives were deleted. This omission made her voice sound as loud as a hundred and two violins stranded in an empty room. Everyone glanced up from their books, calculators, pencil cases, newspapers, magazines, filofaxes, crossword puzzles, microfiche screens, like the big bad wolf huffed and puffed the roof off.

'The red bicycle downstairs, belong to anyone here?'

We all know and have made peace with the fact there are tons, I mean, literally tons of red bicycles in the world. You know this. I know this. There were loads of red bicycles in front of Hackney Central Library that afternoon doing exactly what bicycles have always done. Absorb time in an incredibly, nonchalant manner.

'There's a rip in the seat and the back wheel is covered in mud.'

Settled it. The rip in the seat was wear and tear held in place with strips of Gaffa tape which kept slipping off on account of my bum. As for the mud, well, your girl here was too lazy to clean it and I figured this made my bike less appealing to thieves. The bicycle, the red bicycle was mine. Praise be.

One of the librarians I took to calling Big Bertha because she reminded me of the third level boss in the arcade game *Renegade* (sans fishnet stockings and a crackling whip) approached the shouting girl. She was trying to do this with stealth, moving as slowly as a robot from any old-timey science fiction film you care to mention. I could not hazard a guess as to what Big Bertha intended to do, once she got closer. I raised my right hand high above my head.

The instant I did this a cavalcade of laughter erupted from a cabal of students seated two rows down from me. Their tabletop, I'm not going to lie, a broiling, roiling sea of books and juice cartons they were weren't supposed to consume in the library but did so anyway with breathtaking disregard for the rules. All seven of them had been popping foil the whole time, slurping obscenely through straws, burping and harping on about Pippa Fletcher's chest in *Home & Away*, and toing and froing in back slang about which Shakespeares Sister they would kick out of bed for farting. They stopped arguing in back slang and their voices grew louder and more animated when they spoke about rumoured sightings of Sluggo stickers down Hendon. They also ruined *A Nightmare on Elm Street 3* for me. They revealed Nancy, the heroine from *A Nightmare on Elm Street*, died at the end. I'd been pestering Mum to rent the video. Not that Mum or I were particularly big fans of horror films. I just happened to catch *A Nightmare on Elm Street* on Channel 4 late one Saturday evening and was smitten by Nancy's resourcefulness. This was why I was interested in watching *A Nightmare on Elm Street 3: Dream Warriors*. The smoke-filled trailer put Nancy Thompson's return to the franchise front and centre. No two ways about it, sitting by the windows was proving to be a bad decision. I should have taken my chances on the tables near the counter, with the gossipy librarians exchanging hints 'n' tips about the best Beres Hammond album and deciding who, from their ranks, was best suited to mount the Diwali display.

The girl asking after my bicycle scrunched her eyes and glanced at the group seated at the table. Their laughter ceased. One of the boys – I'm guessing the ring leader – in yellow dungarees, pushed back his chair aggressively before standing up with his chest puffed out. The girl stepped forward with a take no prisoners set to her jaw. Her eyebrows were boomeranged-shaped and looked about ready to fly off her forehead and hit Yellow Dungarees in his throat piece. You could have heard a pin drop. Yellow Dungarees sat down quick with a look on his face like rumpled bedsheets trying to smoke a cigarette. He looked so profoundly confused he stood up again, puffed out his chest like whut-whut before one of his cohorts, with lipstick on her teeth, dragged him back down by tugging on his dungaree pouch with such force, I heard it rip.

Throughout all this Big Bertha had stopped moving and was standing as still as Lot's wife the instant she was turned into a pillar of salt.

'Let's go,' the girl ordered.

Before this girl with hair black as a moth's shadow showed up I'd been reading Chaucer. In pencil, I circled and shaded in the lines, 'To do evil and never hear it spoken of again.' I wasn't entirely sure how these words would help me in the A-level mock exams wheeling around the corner but I'd gone ahead and highlighted them anyway. After devouring Chaucer, I was going to have to tackle Marx and Weber for Sociology which I wasn't looking forward to, at all. There were other things waiting to be read, to be consumed, which said little to me about my life. Add to this I now knew Nancy's ultimate fate. What a waste of such a strong and brilliant character. I was growing despondent and I guess what I'm saying is, it was as if I were being rescued from this mood by this girl, who must have flown up the stairs, to reach me.

It was Black History Month. On the far wall behind plexiglass were these huge colour posters of Toni Morrison, Zora Neale Hurston and, Grace Nichols. Toni, Zora, and Grace watched me. All three women looked amused, humour lingering in their sparkling eyes as we strolled past. It took all my energy and some of tomorrow's strength not to wave at them.

We made our way towards the giant stairs leading to the exit and forecourt where the bicycle racks were stationed. The sliding doors parted for me like no big deal when I stood in front of them.

Swoosh went the sliding doors when I walked through it.

Swoosh went the sliding doors shutting behind me.

The sun's rays fidgeted off our bicycles. Both bicycles shiny. They looked like they'd just been born. Innocent in the worst way. Even my bicycle with its torn seat and mud-splattered back wheel appeared new, resuscitated from years of carelessness by its proximity to Dorothy's bike.

I stood in front of both bicycles with a strange burning sensation in my mouth, like my tongue was all of a sudden, a soldering iron. I figured this was what it must be like to be a dragon, to have a constant source of heat pulsating in your mouth, all the time, every time. A voice filled with fire. The thrill and danger of this made me want to scream. I did not scream, because my voice, flushed with heat, would eradicate the flesh from the girl and throw her botched shadow on the wall.

'What's the hold-up, feeling ways?' the girl standing next to me wanted to know.

'Feelings ways?'

'Uh-huh for locking up my bicycle like there aren't enough

problems in my life.'

Her bicycle was purple. It had a little wicker basket attached to the front with a bee buzzing away inside of it. I can't say why I'd failed to notice it earlier; it was everything my bicycle wanted to be when it grew up. For one it was shop floor clean, had a slender frame that looked like it could hang in an art gallery or some aristocrat's dining room next to a painting by Leonora Carrington. The front derailleur and derailleur pulley was not weighed down and coated with gunk; the valve caps fronted a fluted art deco look. The housing stop, get this, was where it should be, not MIA going on years as was the case with mine. Yep, make no mistake, everything my bike hoped to be, dreamed of being, except maybe the wicker basket; which looked like something Anne from *The Famous Five* would own and best believe, I could not stand Anne from *The Famous Five* which invariably meant my bicycle couldn't stand Anne from *The Famous Five* either or her hypothetical, wicker basket.

The bee was idly circling until the girl reached into the wicker basket and grabbed it. She held it in her right hand. Then she carefully opened her hand like she was offering the bee to me as a gift, a sacrifice. The bee appeared marvellously stunned at its continued ability to draw breath. There was also something decidedly considered to its motion when it realised it could still fly. It hovered between us, anxious to communicate some important bee thought before lighting out for territories unknown. We watched it go.

The girl was standing right next to me like we were waiting for the same bus. Her hands, both of them, were firmly planted on her wide hips like she was a pioneer woman watching the plains for who knows what manner of threat. All she needed was a weather-beaten Stetson and a six-shooter to complete the image. Her dark hair, her hair of deepest black, swirled about her face, caught up its own air current that had nothing to do with what air was doing everywhere else. Her eyes were brown and shiny like pennies in a wishing fountain.

There was a delightful disaster of freckles splashed across her nose, which was pointy. Distractingly aloof which made me think she might have a touch of the hoity-toits about her. I was slightly taller than her. Just the way she stood though, with both hands planted on her scrumptious hips made this little bit of height negligible and circumspect. Difficult to believe in like accounts of dirigibles sailing across Suffolk skies. I liked and enjoyed what I heard of her voice. It sounded historied and long memoried like the mud caught in the serpentine treads on the back wheel of my bicycle.

She was wearing black combat trousers with a truly alarming number of pockets running down the legs. The silver round studs acting as buttons for these pockets caught the light and shone like delinquent stars with no desire for their fall to be softened by wishes. Her T-shirt was mustard gas yellow with blocky black letters on the front which said: *Marathon Suicide Addict*.

It suddenly grew chilly, tattered but resolute ribbons of cold air bossily pushing punctured paracetamol blister packs, bus tickets, shiny crisp packet wrapping and, stray yellow pages from *Loot*, 'the free ads-paper,' across the pavement.

The girl standing next to me didn't appear to mind the cold too tough while I fought the urge to begin rubbing my hands together as though warming them in front of a roaring bonfire. The furnace I felt in my mouth had deserted me and I came this close to stamping my feet to get circulation going.

Hours later, brushing my teeth in front of the bathroom mirror, wincing at the sight of the 1p sized bruise under my right eye, resisting the urge to touch; I would remember really liking the fact the girl had words on her T-shirt. Here was a girl you had to read.

I blinked. I blinked my way back into the world, fully the real world, with people walking by, cars beeping and pieces of litter swirling and forming a little tornado that disintegrated as quickly as it was whipped into existence, with only a floating Safeway's plastic bag, proof positive of what I'd seen, making a daredevil bid for the upper branches of a Cornelian cherry tree. I blinked my way back into the real world and not the world of the interior, where my thoughts darted about like the blue-bellied dragonflies I occasionally caught sight of while making my way through Hackney Marshes. I fumbled for my keys, feeling a tad unnerved by the large metallic Snoopy keyring Mum gave me for my tenth birthday. Snoopy – in his Joe Cool guise – wore a lewd smirk I did not appreciate one bit as I reached for my bike lock with what I truly hoped was laid back, Eartha Kitt cool, which backfired immediately when I dropped my keys and had to pick them up again. I tried to style it out by pretending I hadn't dropped my keys in the first place which was simply ridiculous because I had dropped them and compounded this fact by saying, 'Butterfingers,' to no one in particular.

After rotating the key clockwise, my bike lock came apart. Our bicycles were free. I turned to the girl. Offered my name. She looked me in the eyes directly before asking me to repeat it.

'Pacific Hale,' I said, my hand reaching for hers.

She shook my hand quickly, then reached down to unlock her bicycle. I stepped back. I began futzing with my seat, trying to make it to appear less trampy by smoothing down the frayed strips of Gaffa tape, when the girl, rearing up from releasing her bike lock, elbowed me in my right eye. I slammed my eyes shut. I saw a lone star shimmer in the sudden dark.

'I'm so sorry,' the girl said.

Shocked tears streamed down my face. Snot gushed from my nose. I covered my hurt eye with my right hand.

'I'm so sorry,' she said again.

I flinched my left eye open. I saw the girl moving towards me, her bike lock dangling from her hand like a club. I was backing away, beating a hasty retreat. She was trying to remove my hand so she could access the damage. I was reluctant to have her do so simply because no one had ever placed a star into my head before. I was determined to cling to the star, leaking a crimson shadow. The girl was close enough to lift my hand away. I flinched my right eye open and quickly wiped my streaming nose.

'Ouch,' she said.

'That bad?' I bleated nervously.

'Does it hurt?' she asked.

'Only when I laugh,' I said.

'I'm really sorry I hurt you.'

'My fault,' I said, burping up a saliva spackled sob.

'No way. I should have been more careful,' the girl acknowledged.

'Pphhfttt,' I said sticking out my tongue and blowing on it.

'How bad can it be?' I asked, trying to sound brave.

We were leaning into each other; both her hands were on my shoulders. I was sniffling, mortified by the fact my nose was still running and my right eye throbbed like it had a frying egg for a cornea. The girl was saying something.

'Pardon?' I said.

'The café, over there. There! They'll have ice, can you walk?'

I tried not to laugh when I said, 'Affirmative unless you're planning on clobbering my legs as well.'

'Maybe later,' the girl said.

'Promises promises,' I said to myself. Least ways I thought I said this to myself until the girl said, 'Say again?'

'Nothing,' I said quickly.

'I'm Dorothy,' the girl offered, reaching for the hand I'd protected my eye with. My palm was sticky with water from my one injured eye and nose nought from wiping my nose. She shook my hand anyway.

'Nice to meet you,' I said.

'You sure?' Dorothy asked, guiding me towards the café.

After giving Dorothy my hand time flew by like you

wouldn't believe. Time whizzing by after meandering walks together in any number of parks: Finsbury Park, Bruce Castle Park, Springfield Park, Regent's Park, Hyde Park, Trolley Park, and of course no-name parks, where we played Frisbee. Dorothy making death-defying leaps to catch the hovering disc so I threw the Frisbee higher, faster, just to see what else Dorothy was capable of even though my aim was never going to add to my fame or fortune. Time out of mind playing on sea-saws and swings. Dorothy jumping off her swing at its apex like it was nothing and asking me once she landed to stand guard while she went to pee behind a bush that had a leather skipping rope draped over it. I tried not to listen, pretended not to hear the force with which her pee hit the soil beneath her feet, affecting, I'm sure, its PH levels and any worms unfortunate to be scouting the area. When Dorothy came back there were bramble nicks all over her face.

Time out of mind buying chips and both of us using way too much ketchup so it looked like a gang war was taking place between the saveloy and onion rings. Time out of mind watching episodes of *Press Gang, Round the Twist, Eerie Indiana*, and breaking into the opening theme song for *Maid Marian and Her Merry Men* whenever we skidded into corner shops for supplies and Stanley, sweet Stanley, on those few occasions he came along with us, shaking his head in disbelief as Dorothy and I gangster up the joint by shouting at the top of our voices, 'Damn Fine Marathon bar,' 'Damn Fine Polo mints,' in homage to what was fast becoming our favourite TV show, *Twin Peaks*.

Time out of mind searching for the *Batman Returns* soundtrack on cassette in Our Price and Dorothy making herself disappear by ducking behind one of the freestanding video cassette racks. Me searching for her. Taking my sweet time, glancing up at the ceiling like maybe, just maybe, she's dangling from ceiling hooks. She's not. I ramble on over to the mezzanine where posters and T-shirts for bands like The Cure, Damaged Gods, and Aztec Camera vie for space on the back wall. Nope, she's nowhere near the mezzanine. I extend the drama by marching up to the counter and asking the S-shaped man behind it with mash potatoes teeth and the hesitant beginnings of a goitre, if he's seen her. I describe the black T-shirt she's wearing, with words in white type spelling, *Ancient of Days*, above an enlarged picture of the Michelin Man. I mention her dark hair, dark as two seconds past midnight I say. Her triangular face, like the pyramids in Egypt I say. After ringing up the *Batman Returns* cassette tape and placing it in a creamy white plastic bag, boasting the bright red image of a spinning record, the man standing behind the counter lets me know he hasn't seen anyone matching my description. I thank him for his time. I walk away, ignoring the security guard clocking my every move, getting all screw face like boys did when I destroyed their high score on *Chase H.Q* or completed *Strider* without losing a single life. I draw out the tension by lifting up an issue of *Melody Maker* with Miki Berenyi from Lush on the front cover. If looks could kill the security guard not only killed me, but dug up my body to desecrate. I flick through the pages-la-la-la. When

I'm done I head towards the video racks. I hear Dorothy giggling as she waits to be found.

Time out of mind trying to sneak into *Basic Instincts* and getting caught by the bouffant-haired usherette and having to watch *FernGully* instead. Not giving up on our quest and trying to sneak in again a week or so later and getting nabbed by the same usherette and having to watch *Batman Returns* instead. Dorothy and I making gagging sounds when Batman and Catwoman kiss. Dorothy had a tub of popcorn in her lap. Her mouth busy chewing through the yellow belly of a snake. I reached for the popcorn, Dorothy pulled it away and my hand almost fell in her lap. Dorothy laughed. Her mouth a gack of gummy snake bits. I reach for the popcorn again. I grab a handful, I ate. It wasn't just popcorn though; it was like I was devouring darkness, the darkness in the cinema. The darkness the usherette had to carefully wend her way through with a small torch aiding her progress to the front of the flickering silver screen, where she stood with a tray of sweating ice-cream cups, rows of Fruitella and quietly cooling bottles of Orangina. I looked behind me at the thin beam of light emerging from the projection box. It was as if this ray of light sculpted us. Like somehow everyone sitting in the cinema had their origins in it. I slowly turned away and took another mouthful of popcorn, tasting the sharp bite of salt and I wanted more darkness, more spools of film to be discovered and run through the projector so Dorothy and I could remain sitting next to each other for longer. The usherette, with her tray of confectionary treats held in front of her chest, stood in front of the silver screen with an air of mystical boredom radiating from her face in the way certain stones, filigreed with holes, released air bubbles when dropped in a glass of water. After serving a handful of people she walked away.

On the screen, Batman punched a goon dressed up as a scarecrow. The Ice Princess plummeted to her death. Catwoman released a bird from her mouth. Penguin gored through a fish and Dorothy, her triangular face, stippled with antlered shadows, whispered, 'Stanley's going to have kittens when I tell him we saw this before him,' Dorothy grinned and said, 'almost makes up for getting turfed out of *Basic Instincts*.'

'Almost,' Dorothy repeated as I reached for the tub of popcorn and she pulled it away.

Only this time round there was mournful music accompanying our actions. On the screen, Batman stood brooding while the music surging from the speakers carefully wrapped itself around me. Offering the consolation Batman could not feel. I listened. It was shocking and wonderful what the music was doing to me. It made me feel like I was sinking through the Hadal Zone without the mercy of a tail or even one of those naturally evolved lanterns to entice prey and me, falling through this darkness and flourishing, regardless.

The music dissipates under the diegetic, guttural roar of the Batmobile tearing through Gotham City. For weeks I'd been umming and ahhing trying to decide what the first song on the tape I was making Dorothy should be. As the film reached its denouncement I turned to Dorothy and said, 'We're staying through the credits. I need to know who did the music.' Dorothy looked at me and said, 'Have you've been crying?'

All these marvellous moments smouldering inside us the second Dorothy took my hand in hers in front of Hackney Central Library and my right hand is moving on from that spectacular meeting to the instant I picked up the phone on its second ring so its clamorous tone didn't wake Mum.

I knew it was her.

It could only ever be her.

Dorothy tended to call at night.

I heard.

'Hello Pacific,' like no time had passed at all.

'Hello yourself,' I said, trying not to trip over my tongue which felt oversized and big for nothing.

To say I was overjoyed to hear Dorothy's voice doesn't quite cut it. I thought I would die waiting to hear what she'd say next. I was also filled with tension; my body ragged with it, like how exactly was she going to hurt me next? I bit my bottom lip to make sure I wasn't dreaming.

During the four months Dorothy and I were apart, my dreams, when they arrived, tended to be ill-fated sorties into enemy terrain. Fountains I stumbled past gushed blood. I saw an injured dog limp into a barbed-wire fence. Crows feasted on carrion not entirely of this world, their ebony wings, striking me as attire for a ceremony, I could not stop myself from attending.

I was on the verge of sleep when the telephone rang. There was a part of me that couldn't shake the feeling I was at the start of a dream which would end with blood on my hands.

'What's the matter?' Dorothy asked, 'Mastermind got your tongue?'

'Just really nice to hear your voice,' I said.

Dorothy said nothing.

I looked round my room. There really wasn't much to see, wasn't much going on. I must have pressed a button on the phone strictly by accident because the small light on the phone's face lit up. There was a sense of elated pageantry taking place within the phone's LED display, of soundless rejoice. It had finally brought Dorothy to me, just as I was starting to believe such a thing was impossible. The LED display was pleased with itself, shining, it seemed to me, a little brighter than usual. I have to say the blunt force trauma of hearing Dorothy's voice meant I couldn't fully participate in its joy, its righteous sense of accomplishment.

'How have you been?' I asked.

'Cool as,' Dorothy replied.

'About the joke, if you can even call it that. I mean, yeah? You know? I didn't mean anything by it, I was only...'

'Forget that,' Dorothy said, cutting me off. 'I got upset, overreacted. I'm the one who should be apologising.'

'OK, sure,' I said clicking on my bedside lamp and staring up at the ceiling.

'No really. I'm sorry. It was all in my head,' Dorothy said.

'OK.'

'Yeah?'

'Yeah.'

'Really?'

'Mm.'

'Thanks.'

'I've missed you so much,' I said so quietly I doubted Dorothy heard me.

'I don't even want to think about how many times you must have watched *Adventures in Baby Sitting*,' Dorothy said.

'My favourite film,' I said.

'Your favourite film,' Dorothy repeated.

'Only watched it once,' I said.

'Chatting shit about?' Dorothy said.

'No, really,' I said, 'I didn't even want to, Mum made me.'

'I bet your mum hates me now.'

'Don't be silly,' I said.

'You know what? It's funny. Never really thought about it till now. The main actress and I almost have the same surname.' Dorothy's voice sounded like she was tilting her head up and a little to her right, to better absorb this revelation.

'Coincidence,' I said, 'it doesn't mean anything.'

'I should have phoned.'

'It's fine,' I said.

'If you say so,' Dorothy replied.

I nodded, then remembered Dorothy couldn't see me nodding so I said, 'I do.'

'What about music,' Dorothy asked, changing the subject, 'heard any new songs?'

The last time I paid attention to music was when I heard the stray lines of a Ray Charles song blasting out a van speeding by her house. Ray Charles was singing about Georgia being on his mind. Two days later, while doing the dishes, I mentioned the song to Mum. I asked if Georgia was a person or place. Mum didn't reply. She was too busy staring at a scatter of soap bubbles floating by with the exact same look she had in her eyes whenever Dad, with a sly smile, shook sawdust from his hair. Do I have to say, I remember the sawdust being as shiny as King Nebuchadnezzar's the second's beard?

'You listening, did you hear me?' Dorothy asked.

'Yes, I heard you and no, just old stuff, I haven't heard anything new. You?'

'Nah, nothing worth writing home about,' Dorothy said. 'What about books, read anything recently?'

'Not really,' I said.

'Seriously? That doesn't sound like you.'

'Nothing caught my eye,' I replied.

I was sitting up in bed trying to picture where Dorothy was. Could be she was downstairs in the sunroom, crammed with cardboard boxes filled with old Maths tests. Her father was a home-school Maths tutor for an outfit called Wonder Maths with its main office in Islip. I still have one of their business cards kicking round here someplace. The Proportionality symbol was their corporate logo, embossed right in the centre of the card.

Dorothy's father gave me the card on my first visit, dunno, maybe second? He had these really sad, baggy eyes and barely said more than two words to me whenever I came round, which thinking about it now makes me wonder if it was him who gave me the business card in the first place.

Please understand he wasn't rude, just uninterested. He was like somebody whose existence was a small cough politely excusing itself.

Dorothy's mother on the other hand was exuberantly vibrant like a sway of road bound for glory. A road; kings, queens, wizards, witches, griots, troubadours, viziers, and soothsayers were buried under. She was flamboyantly loose-limbed, wore floaty clothes more suited to the tropics. She was forever and a day asking questions about school, my mother, books I was reading. I would eagerly release books from my rucksack for her inspection. It didn't matter what the books were: *Her Privates We, Tess of the D'Urbervilles, Old Soldiers Never Die, Mrs. Frisby and the Rats of Nimh, The Basketball Game, The Strange Case of William Whipper-Snapper, Ratatat! The Collected Bruce Bairnsfather* (she wrongly assumed Stanley would enjoy due to the illustrations) Mrs. Shu always handled them with such patient care I began to feel bad.

I was incredibly careless with books. I underlined passages in pencil like it was going out of style. Dog-eared pages like it was a legacy I was born to. I wrote an unwieldy amount of notes in the margins and squished bugs pancake-flat if they dared land on the pages for a moment's rest. The squashed bodies of these bugs becoming part of a new alphabet I watched Mrs. Shu slowly run her fingers along, trying, I think, to get closer to the mystery. The elusive meaning these squandered bits of thorax, abdomen and wings, added to the narrative.

Like her daughter, Mrs. Shu had exquisite brown eyes

which were sometimes scarily bright. Craggy lines quivered around them whenever she smiled and revealed a sizeable gap between her front teeth. Her hair, while still black, lacked the narcotic sheen of Dorothy's hair.

Looking back, I guess it would be fair to say I was a little enchanted by Dorothy's mum. I loved how her voice (especially when she was singing along with the radio or shouting out answers during *Catch Phrase* with Roy Walker) sounded. It had a breathy, melodic lilt and her laugh! Oh, my days. Best believe she had this great, big, really big, stupendous laugh which sucked you right in, encouraged you to take pleasure in what she found amusing. I must confess I have a little difficulty recalling her ever staying still. Not in the front room filled with its careworn light and sheets of paper waiting to be marked on the big glass table. She barely remained stationary in the kitchen. Frequently moving from the black mica countertop to get something spherical from the massive fridge which, no joke, could easily have had my fridge for dinner with room left for afters.

Mrs. Shu was from Malaysia like her husband and came to England at the tail end of the 1950s to train as a nurse. She spoke about these times with an air of illicit wonder, as though it wasn't so much her own life, she recounted, but that of a beloved aunt, who in time became the subject of scandalous gossip. I listened avidly while she spoke about the tiny box room she lodged in at Bromley, a three-bar electrical heater her constant companion. She regaled us with wonder tales of what it was like to walk the London streets in the 60s, the sudden chaos of mini-skirts, sex and insurrection sparkling in the air like the fireflies she cupped in her hands when she was small. Mrs. Shu also spoke of fog-bound mornings which made me think of the fog-saturated moors in *The Hound of the Baskervilles*. She made mention of trees with boreholes big enough to climb in.

She once described seeing a Hmong tribesman standing outside a Dry Cleaners called, Pressed to Impress, in New Cross Gate. She explained he was such a remarkable sight she did not believe he was real. What exactly were the chances she would see a member of the Hmong dressed in a finely embroidered short shirt with an exquisite pink sash wrapped around his waist? He was living dangerously; pink was not a colour she saw many men wearing. She waved at him from the top deck of the bus. Fronds of smoke curling from the lit cigarette of the passenger sitting behind her steamed up the glass, the reason, she explained, her wave was not returned.

With my legs crossed at my ankles, I sat on the edge of my seat whenever Dorothy's mother spoke about her past, while Dorothy, rolling her eyes, kicked my feet under the kitchen table before telling her mum not to exaggerate.

'Why does everyone go on and on and Ariston about the 60s, they weren't all that.'

'You are correct one hundred percent,' her mother said. 'They were so much more and so much less.'

'What does that even mean?' Dorothy asked, throwing her hands skyward in mock exasperation which became real exasperation by the time her hands returned to her lap. 'Can you please explain why you Miyagi out whenever Pacific's here? Mum, did you hear what I just said? Mum, Mum?'

'That advert hasn't been on in ages,' Stanley said, looking up from his *Cloak & Dagger* comic.

'Another country heard from,' Dorothy said in a huff.

'What advert?' Mrs. Shu asked, dicing onions on a wooden chopping board with a sharp knife. I heard *Ssk Sssk*.

'Hang on a sec, how come you reply to him?' Dorothy asked pointing towards Stanley with an imperious tilt of her chin. 'That's sexist or something, right Pacific?'

I heard *Krr Krg Rgg* as Mrs. Shu used a pistil and mortar to grind up black pepper.

'All I said is the Ariston advert hasn't been on in ages,' Stanley replied, shooting me a quick wink.

I heard *Shk Shk Shk* as Mrs. Shu sliced up capsicums.

'Is that a joke?' Dorothy asked.

'You're right, I haven't seen it in while,' Mrs. Shu added. 'The one with the washing machine and people dancing around it, correct?'

I heard *Krssh Krssh* as Mrs. Shu, waiting for a reply, sliced through oyster mushrooms.

'And a fridge, there's a fridge in the advert too,' Dorothy said, stretching with the tips of her fingers for a slice of onion on the chopping board. Dorothy reached for the chopping board with a look of determination on her face I knew well from watching her chase down my banana throws of the Frisbee. I watched her fingers flex, skirting the invisible, until, she had a slice of onion in her hand. She dashed it at Stanley, who took his sweet time peeling it off his red school blazer and when he was done sniffing at it inquisitively, Stanley ate it.

'Nasty business,' Dorothy said with a shudder.

I heard *Brssh Brrshhh* as Mrs. Shu filled a glass up with water.

'How did you and Mr. Shu meet?' I asked. I was caught up in the energy in the kitchen, which seemed to permit anything, even me asking a private question.

'They met in a post office,' Dorothy said with a yawn.

'Where do you think old adverts go?' Stanley asked philosophically. He placed his comic down on the table. The cover showed the superhero and superheroine Cloak and Dagger being viciously manhandled by an old man. The old man's human parts—excluding his undernourished face—had fallen into obsolescence and were replaced with shiny, hydraulic, hunks of metal. From the look of things, Cloak and Dagger were about to bite the farm. Cloak's costume was in tatters, and Dagger, possibly unconscious, was being held up by tangled strands of her blond hair. Stanley would have lent me the comic, for sure, if I asked for it, and maybe if I had asked and had the opportunity to read it, I would better understand why I found that cover so alluring but I wasn't into comics, despite Stanley's frequent attempts to get me to read them. Whenever Stanley suggested I read one of his comics, I said, 'Nah, you're alright.'

The trails and tribulations facing Cloak and Dagger were far from my mind when I said, 'Oh,' trying to keep disappointment from creeping into my voice because the place Mrs. Shu and Mr. Shu met was boring.

Mrs. Shu, smiling at me with a faraway look in her eyes said, 'Yīnyuè is correct, her father and I met in a post office.'

Mrs. Shu was about to hand the glass of water to Stanley. For some reason, I thought it was for me and reached for it. I thanked her and took a swig, exaggerating the throat work some as I eagerly glugged the contents down. Stanley got up and poured himself a glass of water. He returned to his seat.

'Give me a break,' Dorothy said, staring at her mum and then rolling her eyes all over again. Stanley after taking a sip, splutter coughed like the water had gone down the wrong pipe. Dorothy leapt up and thumped Stanley on the back and when she was done thumping him up but good, she tickled him under his armpits. Stanley laughed his loud and somewhat abrasive laugh. He tried to hide his teeth by covering his mouth with his hand but he was a little bit too slow and I saw his teeth. By the time Dorothy sat down, Stanley had stopped laughing and was watching his sister point a remote control at the television my memory has resting on top of the fridge, which, considering the height of the fridge doesn't seem plausible. Anywho, there was definitely a TV in the kitchen and when Dorothy aimed the control at it, *The Krypton Factor* came on.

'Dorrie switch it off, we'll be eating soon,' Mrs. Shu advised. I heard *Shruush* as she turned on the gas under a frying pan lustrous with peanut oil.

'I was hoping for *Treasure Hunt*,' Dorothy said.

'That's on Sundays on Channel Four,' her mother replied, lighting a match.

'Is that a joke?' Dorothy said.

'Ariston and on and on,' Stanley said repeating the jingle from the Ariston advert.

'And on and on and on,' I took up in a slight delirium, pushing my words recklessly close to gibberish.

'Get a room,' Dorothy said, as her mother moved from the cooker to the fridge.

If Dorothy was not in the sunroom, the kitchen, or front room then she had to be in her bedroom with its magnificent row of soft-bellied toys on the long shelf floating above her bed. Posters of T'Pau, Bros, Bananarama, New Kids On The Block, Ya Kid K, and Cantopop sensation, Beyond, plastered all over her bedroom walls. There was a staid benevolence in the theatricality of their poses I always found myself making fun of and exaggerating whenever I was in Dorothy's bedroom. Dorothy, vaguely amused by my pantomime, the pouting lips, vague stares into the middle distance, freely admitted these posters were good for one thing and one thing only. Triggers for her masturbation sessions.

'Sessions?' I said.

Say for me I had one massive black and white poster on my bedroom wall of Ian Curtis from Joy Division sitting on an amplifier, head bowed, fingers bracing his eyes shut, during a soundcheck at The Moonlight Club, the legend goes. This poster, the perfect image of dejection did not easily lend itself to masturbatory fantasies.

'Holy shit,' Dorothy exclaimed when she saw the poster for the first time. I remember feeling a peculiar sense of elation swim right through me when I heard disbelief rupture

Dorothy's voice and I'm telling you right here, right now, if Mastermind hadn't chosen that particular moment to let rip a fusillade of farts, I believe, emboldened by the dark courage of Joy Division songs, combined with the simple, unbelievable fact we were in my bedroom I would have pulled Dorothy close to me and kissed her, point-blank, on the mouth. Biting and drawing blood from her lips like Sylvia Plath did when she kissed Ted Hughes for the first time ever. Mastermind's fart distracted me, kept me from swiftly reacting to the slight shift in how Dorothy perceived me. Pointing at the poster Dorothy said.

'That's never Glen Medeiros.'

'Not on your life,' I said.

'You have strange tastes.'

'Strange as some but not as strange as others,' I said.

Mastermind chose this moment to fart again. Clenching her nostrils shut with two fingers in close to perfect mimicry of how Ian Curtis pinched his eyes shut, Dorothy said in a muffled voice, 'There's something seriously wrong with your cat.'

Mastermind gave Dorothy a truly awful look. I figured it would be a good idea to pick Mastermind up to calm him down, even though he was never, I repeat, never, the kind of cat to tolerate being held for very long. Besides, he had stink bum so I allowed him.

'You sure have a lot of books,' Dorothy said, removing her fingers from her nose and surveying the books jutting up like stalagmites from the floor. 'A shit ton of military history,' she added with a faint air of suspicion.

'Those belonged to Dad,' I said.

'Oh,' Dorothy said.

'I like reading,' I added defensively.

'Words, words, words.' Dorothy said.

'Are good for you,' I said.

'If you say so,' Dorothy replied, plunking herself down on my bed and pulling my pillow over her lap. My heart did a backflip and my mouth went dry. It took a couple of seconds for me to remember I left the tape I was making her in the double-deck cassette player in the front room downstairs. Relief flooded my face and made me feel a little lightheaded as Dorothy scooted forward and made like she was about to dash the pillow at Mastermind. She decided against this fatal course of action by returning the pillow to her lap which was incredibly lucky for her. As a reward for his continued restraint, I reached down and gently stroked Mastermind's eyelids. I felt the jellied give of his eyeballs under my fingertips as Mastermind, purred.

'Cat has issues,' Dorothy said.

Mastermind farted again.

'Urgggggggggggggggh,' Dorothy said, her eyes tearing.

I couldn't believe it. Dorothy Shu was in my bedroom. On my bed, right next to me. I slept in here. Dreamt in here, farted, cried, and picked my nose in here. I drank hot Ribena under the covers after brushing my teeth because why not? I got dressed and undressed here. Listened to music in here, my afro comb with its upraised fist design, transmogrified into a microphone because I willed it so. Out of boredom I sometimes tried to shatter my reputedly, shatter-resistant ruler against my headboard because why not? I fumed and plotted grim vendettas against Mum when she refused to rent A *Nightmare on Elm Street 3: Dream Warriors* for me in here.

I also worked on Dorothy's compilation tape here. I was drawing a cover on the J-card, which, let me tell you, was supposed to look like two shopping trolleys in front of palm trees but the cross-hatching for the palm trees was getting seriously out of hand and the shopping trolleys, without conscious overtures to anthropomorphism on my part, looked apprehensive, as if they were waiting to be used as roller-skates by a giant.

My bedroom. Dorothy Shu was in my bedroom. I wanted to show off; read her a poem, execute a wobble-free handstand and then put some music on. After being suitably mesmerised by my excellent tastes, Dorothy and I would dance together. The sensual elasticity of Olive Oyl's limbs suddenly ours as we spun each other round and round, gracefully avoiding the minefield of books piled up on the floor.

And yet for all this, the brilliant toe scrunching wonder of Dorothy being in my bedroom, another feeling steadily crept into me; the desire for Dorothy to be gone. My bedroom, my sanctuary really, felt smaller and cramped with her in it. I suddenly saw dust bunnies making eyes at me from the skirting boards. I realised how shabby the tower of books on my floor looked, nothing at all like the brave paladins I regarded them to be. There were far too many of them, not only taking up space on my floor but on shelves near my bedroom door. The fact there were so many, an infestation really, hinted at some pathology I didn't have the headspace to explore as the smell of Indian food filled the air.

This smell lingered in my bedroom from when Mum and I first moved in. We tried to combat it by painting the walls, leaving the window open, changing the carpet, and then painting the walls again. The smell would retreat for months at a time, then return with a vengeance. The smell wasn't unpleasant. It was not knowing its origins that caused concern. Dorothy hadn't mentioned the smell yet and I knew from experience opening the window would do little to deter it. Besides, my bedroom window was already open.

Dorothy and I stared at the poster of Ian Curtis. It was massive; taking up the entire north-facing side of my bedroom wall. I saw, like I was seeing this for the very first time, how incredibly careworn it was, all four edges frayed and pockmarked with oily Blu-Tack stains which had seeped through its underside. The poster was too ostentatious a grab at adult sophistication, a desperate clutching at feelings I did not fully understand with poor Ian Curtis as a stand-in for these feelings. I truly believed the poster helped explain me to the world, eked out a territory I could feel safe in. With Dorothy in my bedroom, I suddenly wanted to tear the poster down, feeling somewhat embarrassed by its scale, its on the nose grandiosity.

The bruise below my right eye began throbbing. Not enough to make me bring attention to it by touching it. Still, there must have been some duplicity on my body's part, some enigmatic frequency Dorothy picked up on, because she said, 'Still hurts, doesn't it?'

'What?' I asked.

'Your eye.'

Dorothy was wearing a cream white Bart Simpson T-shirt. Instead of Bart being his usual, patented yellow self, Bart was black, with shoulder-length dreadlocks. He was pulling back on his obviously Tom Sawyer, inspired slingshot. There was a big stone in the middle, aimed at the onlooker. Dorothy was also wearing tartan black and red, drainpipe trousers. Her whole ensemble goof troop at first blush. However, this initial impression dissolved when you paid attention to the skinny, lilac, trouser suspenders. The left one hung loosely off her left shoulder with a febrile, offbeat sensuality which made looking at it difficult. The black and red tartan drainpipe trousers were just a little too short so I saw the pale skin of Dorothy's legs when she bounced the heels of her feet against the side of my bed which made Mastermind stare at her like he wanted to claw her eyes out.

Dorothy's breath smelt of apple flavoured Hubba Bubba chewing gum which made perfect sense since we'd been chewing this brand while meandering about Stoke Newington, more specifically Osbaldeston Road. We overtook two Haredi kids on Cazenove. They were carrying leather bound books in fancy Ziploc plastic bags and you know me, I was craning my neck into last week trying to read the titles when Dorothy suggested going to The Waste. I was all, that sounds cool, not paying close attention to what Dorothy said because my eyes were locked and loaded on the books when she shouted, 'Allow that,' loud enough to ruffle the two Haredi boys, who quickly crossed the road, without looking.

Cars beeped their horns and I heard screeching tyres. Despite the anguished sounds, these boys made it to the other side of the road, without a single scratch on them while Dorothy and I, if we continued on our meandering trajectory would eventually reach Upper Clapton Road, concussed and bleeding under the yoke of its new sobriquet, Murder Mile.

Dorothy, lowering her voice, explained we were not going to The Waste, because distance, and not only that but The Waste would be chocker with shoppers hunting the stalls for bargains and who really needs that noise? Not us. We decided to explore London Fields instead, and were making our way there when I heard myself say, 'Forget this for a laugh, let's just go to mine.' A suggestion I was now beginning to regret.

Dorothy was staring at my *Oliver & Company* pillowcase. She ran both hands over Oliver's whiskers and Mastermind, resting at my feet, shivered.

'Your favourite cartoon?' Dorothy asked.

'Sometimes,' I said.

I was about to stand up and recommend we hit the bricks. Go for a walk, there was a park near me or maybe we could head for London Fields sameway or catch the tube to Trocadero in the West End where we could chase each other in bumper cars and time permitting, take a gander at arcade machines, when Dorothy said.

'My favourite is *Pinocchio*, the Disney one with the sharp-faced fox and sleepy-eyed cat. Can't recall their names. They absolutely terrified me as a kid. I mean a fox, a cat, big deal right? Wrong! The fact they were wearing clothes, really scared me. Their... I don't know if you remember this, if you've even seen the cartoon but, their, I'm sure, their clothes didn't fit them properly, hung loosely off their bodies and I couldn't shake the feeling they stole the clothes from dead bodies. I used to jump behind the settee whenever they appeared. I still watched the screen though, through my fingers, like this.'

Dorothy placed her left hand on my face and carefully spread her fingers apart. Her finger, the little one, came dangerously close to touching the bruise. So close in fact I have a memory of her actually touching it, of me blinking back tears, which didn't happen, didn't take place. Isn't it strange, how tenderness, the memory of tenderness can sometimes amount to nothing more but talk of bruises?

After splitting my room into segments so it looked strange and unfamiliar to me, Dorothy gently removed her hand from my face. My room returned to its standard size.

'I didn't like how they moved, the cat, the fox, could be my memories are miffed and playing tricks on me. I'm sure there's a scene where the animation glitches and the two of them, the cat, the fox, I can't remember their names; were speeded up. Could be there was something wrong with the tape and I was too frightened to mess with the V-hold button on the TV. Who knows? Either way, I couldn't keep myself from wondering how they met. The cat. The fox. What circumstance of fate brought these two together?'

'I don't know,' I said.

'Why would you?' Dorothy snapped. 'I suspect it was something felonious, that the right word?' she asked softly, trying to regain her composure.

'It is,' I said.

'Thanks,' Dorothy said.

'You're welcome,' I said.

Dorothy continued. 'I've always believed the cat and fox shared a secret, something horr... felonious they'd done together. That's why they're stuck with one another. That's why they're wearing clothes. Disguises to keep them from the long arm of the law. It's them, the two of them, wondering about them, being terrified by them, which makes *Pinocchio* my favourite cartoon even though I haven't seen it in ages.'

'That so?' I asked.

'Uh-huh. But growing up I had this *Disney Story A Day* book published during the year I was born. Mum got it for me. She pulled a copycat crime and bought one for Stanley the year he was born. Each page had a story starring Disney characters for every day of the year.'

'Like Minnie Mouse and Donald Duck?' I asked eagerly.

'Calm down, calm down. Not just flagship characters. Chip and Dale were there, the crows from Dumbo, Gyro Gearloose.'

'He's in *DuckTales*,' I gurgled a little too excitedly.

'I swear if you begin singing the *DuckTales* opening theme I'll scream. So yeah these books had Disney characters living their everyday lives, going about their everyday business. Guess which Disney characters had their story unfold on my birthday?'

'No way,' I said.

'Fucking A,' Dorothy whispered.

'You're scaring me,' I said. 'Are you sure I can't sing the *DuckTales* opening theme to, you know, combat my fear?'

'Yes. On Stanley's birthday, in my book, was a Winnie-the-Pooh story with Tigger being fabulous. In Stanley's book, on his birthday, a King Louie story where King Louie finds and puts on a pair of shoes. In both books, on my birthday, were stories featuring the fox and cat from *Pinocchio*. In Stanley's book, they go on a ride in a stolen hot air balloon. In my book, they kidnap Cleo, Pinocchio's goldfish.'

'Blow me down,' I said as Mastermind purred because he heard the word, "fish."

'That's my favourite cartoon,' Dorothy said, handing me back my pillow. The pillow was a riot of crumple zones because she'd pressed and folded it against her body while speaking.

'I still can't believe I hurt your eye,' she said.

'It's fine, trust.'

'Still,' she said.

'Not like you did it on purpose,' I said.

'Still,' Dorothy said, pulling her left suspender brace over her shoulder.

'*Treat me nice/treat me good/treat me/like you know/ you should/cause I'm not made of wood and I don't have a wooden heart*,' I sang, hugging my pillow.

'Cheap blow, guess that's what I get for not letting you sing *DuckTales*,' Dorothy said.

I nodded my head vigorously until it looked like my head

was in danger of falling off. Dorothy stared at me until we both burst out laughing. We hugged each other. The pillow didn't offer as much as a whimper as it got crushed between us. Mastermind left out of our embrace, acted like he didn't give a spit, by swiping the edge of my duvet with his paws.

'I've never told anyone that,' Dorothy said.

'The cartoon yeah?'

'Why it's my favourite.'

'So we share a secret?'

'Yes and another.'

'We do?'

'Uh-huh, you can't sing for shit.'

'I can't?'

'I love hearing you sing anyway.'

'You do?'

'*Life is like a hurricane/deep in Duckberg,*' Dorothy sang, slowly releasing me.

'*Might solve a mystery/or rewrite history/Ducktales!/ Whoooh oh,*' Dorothy and I sang together.

We were loud enough to unsettle Mastermind who took a running dash over my bed and leapt out my bedroom window. Because Mastermind is spectacular and wherever there's a cat there's a miracle he landed on his feet as Mum came knocking on my door. Mum, emboldened by the presence of a stranger, totally forget herself and pushed my door open without giving me a chance to answer. Mum and I would share words about this later, but right then, I was busy and Dorothy was busy, looking at Mastermind staring back at us before making his way to unleash havoc or perhaps discover some modicum of peace amongst the petunias, nasturtiums and jasmine in the next-door neighbour's garden.

'What are you two looking at,' Mum asked.

'It's a secret,' I said.

'What's that smell?' Dorothy asked.

I was in my bedroom. Dorothy was on the phone. Mum was fast asleep. Where Mastermind was, I couldn't say. Dorothy still hadn't spoken so I did.

'Everything good?'

'Cool and the gang,' Dorothy said. 'What you up to?'

'Not much,' I said.

'Great,' Dorothy replied her voice brimming with intrigue, 'need you for something.'

You should have seen me. Leaping out of bed, getting dressed with the frenetic speed of Roadrunner, wait a sec, Roadrunner doesn't wear clothes, Speedy Gonzales. I grabbed Dorothy's tape. It wasn't finished by a long shot. There was room for at least one more song on Side B and I still hadn't settled on a title. The tape's cover was laughable and don't get me started on the palm trees. No matter. I would take the tape with me and place it in Dorothy's hands.

I brushed my teeth with a ghoulish smile slapped on my face. The smile lingered, stretching past the respectable until I splashed my face with cold water to make double sure there was no sleep milk lingering in my eye corners. Mum was fast asleep in her room and I kept sighing with relief because the phone ringing hadn't woken her up.

I left a note on my pillow, explaining I was going to see Dorothy. I drew a smiley face at the end of my words to assuage any misgivings Mum might have. As I quietly closed the front door behind me, I saw Mastermind making his way towards the kitchen. I blew him a kiss. Mastermind looked at me like yeah yeah I see you but so what?

Dorothy lived about forty-five minutes away. I was far too excited and way too impatient to wait for the night bus. I started running. I ran all the way there. I didn't know I could do it until I did. I ran. Under a brilliantly black sky scrubbed free of clouds.

I ran. Heart pounding in my mouth. I ran, my ankles groaning in protest. I ran. Past trembling shop fronts. I ran past a man bellowing, 'I don't know you from Adam. I don't know you from my twelfth pube. I don't know you from Adam.' The man looked difficult and rough. His skin the braised white of orange pith. He had a Father Christmas beard the colour of lumpy custard with no jolly *Ho ho ho!* to it, at all. He was standing next to a bus shelter. Inside the bus shelter's backlit glass frame was a poster for an exhibition at The National Portrait Gallery called: Under Skin. The poster was an anterior drawing of the human skull. I heard the man shout, 'I don't know you from Adam,' at the skull. What the skull said back, I can hardly guess.

I ran. Past parked cars, their windscreen and windscreen wipers speckled with the dust of the dreaming city. I ran past eviscerated telephone boxes sighing ditties which attracted foxes unlucky in love for now and possibly for always.

I ran past a drunk with burst capillaries like a splurge of

war paint on her face. After spilling brown liquid from a can of Heineken on the ground, she wavered about some before settling down to her knees with guileless grace, as though she were re-enacting the illustration next to the nursery rhyme about Little Miss Muffet, seconds before the plucky spider put the kibosh on Little Miss Muffet's peaceful consumption of 'curds and whey'.

With one tooth in her head, she got busy with the holy work of planting paper flowers in pavement cracks. I stopped running. I watched her. I couldn't see where she got the flowers from. I did see her peel back her chapped, cosmopolitan lips, to reveal the sole misbegotten tooth in her mouth. I watched her kiss the blocky stem of a paper flower. She offered me this flower, by lifting it towards my throat. I took the paper flower and placed it in my waistcoat pocket.

Can I say, minutes later I wished for this woman an enfilade of rooms filled with music made by ney flutes, ouds, and Armenian duduks. For specificity and beauty's sake, I wished for these rooms to be in Vienna and for each one to be lit by crystal chandeliers. I would love to be able to say this. To reassure myself there was something within me that reached out to her generosity. I would like to say if I wasn't out of breath and already moving away I would have stopped and asked the woman if she needed my help. No. At the time I did not think of any of this. Even my thanks was rushed, spiked with confusion due to her burst hoover bag smell and the single tooth festering in her top gum. I kept running. Knowing at this velocity, this speed, suddenly and egotistically mine the flower would fall out.

I ran past a lamppost with a green flyer attached at eye level and the words, 'Paws for Thought.' The flyer was an advert for a missing cat. The cat in the faded photograph looked like Mastermind. Could very well have been Mastermind, but wasn't Mastermind because Mastermind is a black cat and this cat near enough his twin, was as white as the Milky Bar Kid, with paws that looked like the cat had stepped in a paint roller tray filled with black paint.

I ran past a group of teens, searching for the heart of Saturday night even though it was Thursday solid. One of the teens was wearing a 'Sluggo the Suffering Black Boy,' T-shirt. These shirts were notorious for revealing intricate pencil drawings of a black boy, his face warped and vibrating in agony, as he was shot, stabbed, stomped, choked, garrotted. These images, the work of an anonymous artist, began life as triptych street stickers. Bandits with steam irons roamed the city streets and peeled these stickers from walls and the backs of traffic lights as soon as they appeared with an eye to sell them on to collectors. The teen wearing the T-shirt had an air of defiance about him, as though any catastrophe the world had to offer, Sluggo, had already absorbed and saved him from. I did not trip or stumble over the wolf whistle the teen in the Sluggo T-shirt aimed at me as I ran past him and his three-man crew huddled near the doorway of a squat video shop called, Dramaturgy of the Reel. There were posters for the films: *Action Jackson, 976-Evil, Baby Boom, Firewalker, The Monster Squad, Shogun Assassin* and *Just Another Girl*

On The I.R.T stuck to the broad glass front of the video shop. The girl on the poster for *Just Another Girl On The I.R.T.* had tidy braids I would love to have myself someday. A friend of the teen in the Sluggo T-shirt was not only standing in front of the video shop doorway, he also had a *Knight Rider* radio remote car he kept sending to a traffic island marooned in the centre of the road. The toy car drove under the belly of real cars until a sickening crunch made me shiver. I heard someone yell with rapturous delight, 'Iiee iiee iiee iiee look what you've gone and done.'

I kept running. I nearly ran into a stout man walking a wounded dog. I ran under a white woman with hair as blond as a Lichtenstein heroine. She was blowing smoke rings with 1940s stoicism through a 1970s sash window. I saw the tip of her cigarette glow as she waved at me like she'd known me my whole life. I turned up Dorset Road. Some of the houses I dashed past had lights on behind curtained windows like smears of Utterly Butterly. Some didn't. One window had a scraggy, silver foil helium balloon pressed up against it. The balloon must have been a number at some point in its existence. It was difficult to tell what this number had been because the window frame kept most of the balloon from view. I ran past it without a second look.

Years later, tracing my fingers along the silk moiré endpapers of a book or when I'm about to stomp a loop pedal for being all sicky-sicky-bang-bang instead of being a loop pedal and providing harmonic resonance thank you very much, I find myself pondering what that number could have been. I was only young back then, with no idea of what would haunt me and if I could choose, I'd choose never to have seen any part of that silver foil balloon on my way to Dorothy's.

I continued running until I reached Dorothy's door. I knocked on it, easy as. Too out of breath and loved up and happy and out of breath and loved up and overjoyed and heart beating super fast in my chest and the back of my neck to feel any sense of apprehension just the blissful wonder, soon, soon, I'd be seeing her. Breathing her air.

Dorothy yanked the door open as I was pulling my hand back to have another go.

'That's quick,' she said.

'Borrowed Hermes's sandals,' I said, voicing the first thought in my head like a plonker from morning.

'Looks like you borrowed his clothes too, well his grandad's.'

'I ran all the way here,' I managed to say, after gulping down mouthfuls of air.

'Say it don't spray it,' Dorothy replied.

The hallway light was on. Dorothy was lit by this light. For a while I couldn't see her properly. She was just a blurry human-sized shape. Until my eyes slowly adjusted.

Dorothy.

She was wearing a long-sleeved white T-shirt with a charcoal drawing of a cityscape. Under the city, in flowery-script where the words, *"This Isn't Hell, But You Can See It From Here."*

Dorothy had on blue jeans which appeared brand new, freshly minted from some refinery dedicated solely to the colour blue.

Cookie monster blue. Persian blue. Ocean blue. Blue movie blue. Misty blue. Gunmetal blue. Ice pop blue. Planet Earth blue. Peacock feather blue. Bic biro blue. Carbon paper blue.

There was a silver bangle on her left wrist. I'd never known Dorothy to wear bangles. She smelt fantastic, like how you would imagine an angel's neck or foot-bottom smelling. She looked absolutely beautiful, as though in my absence she had discovered a whole new category of beauty, one which barely kept her tethered to the ground.

Her beauty made me want to die.

I could not look at her for very long. I felt ungainly and leaden. Like Cro-Magnon woman standing next to my mother. My face was dripping with copious amounts of sweat. I was breathing heavily despite those mouthfuls of air I mentioned earlier. The clothes I'd chosen in a careless delirium; a glowing white shirt with folksy sleeves, black corduroy trousers, and a magenta waist-coat, felt excessively baroque like I was trying and failing to look like Tasmin Archer in the music video for the song, *Sleeping Satellite*. The shirt with its porcelain buttons was sticking to me in ways that weren't friendly or polite while the waistcoat felt like it had vindictively shrunk two sizes.

Dorothy though.

Oh. My. Days.

Dorothy. Elevated to some other portal I could not venture through, yet somehow, in spite of this, here I was, magically, miraculously, standing in front of her, contravening all known laws of probability, breathing in her air. Not dreaming about it, hoping or imagining; but actually doing it, for real. Dorothy had a single purple hibiscus in her hair. It was there, starry-eyed and open like a wound. Taking in everything.

'Stop staring,' Dorothy said.

I did not say a word. Afraid if I spoke, I would choke on my reply. This was the perfect moment to give Dorothy her present. I discreetly reached into my right trouser back pocket for her compilation tape. It wasn't there. I patted my left trouser pocket. It wasn't there. I must have left it in my bedroom. I reached for the paper flower in my waistcoat pocket as a substitute. It wasn't there either. I suppose the reason for the wolf whistle from the teen in the Sluggo T-shirt. He must have seen it fall and was trying to get my attention. On my life, I went searching for the flower a day or two later.

Dorothy pivoted to her right. I stepped in.

Dorothy's mother was standing at the top of the stairs. She was standing still which I found a little alarming. She waved at me. Hadn't someone done this already? I'd never been in their home this late and every gesture Dorothy and her mother made appeared slurred and sluggish as though taking place under phantom leagues of water.

'Hello Mrs. Shu,' I said recklessly loud with happiness.

'Hello, are you feeling better?'

I shot a glance at Dorothy who pretended to stub away at something on the carpet with her left foot. She was wearing red monkey boots with yellow shoelaces.

'Dorothy mentioned you've been ill. Nothing serious I hope.'

'No, just a bug knocking me for six, then seven, eight, nine,' I said, wincing inwardly at how easily the lie left my lips.

'Such a head for numbers this bug,' Mrs. Shu offered with such a warm smile I still don't fully understand what kept me from leaping up the stairs and hugging the dear, sweet life out of her.

'I feel better knowing she's with you,' Mrs. Shu said.

Dorothy was glaring at me intently while I went about nodding my head like one of those wobbly-headed toys on the dash of cars.

'Have a good evening or is it morning already?' Mrs. Shu said with a sharp laugh, which sounded strange, heavier than it should have, and seemed to go on long after she'd closed her mouth and continued studying me like she couldn't quite place what I was doing in her home at such an outlandish hour.

'I sincerely hope we see more of you and I get the chance to fatten you up,' Mrs. Shu said, placing a hand on the varnished wood of the banister handrail. I thought she was going to walk down the stairs, descend slowly like royalty, like the ideal fairy-tale heroine. She stayed still, looking at us. The way she stared though, like she was caught in a sad reflection made me want to hug her all over again.

'Good night Mum,' Dorothy said pointedly.

'Night girls,' Mrs. Shu said.

Her choice of words, "Night girls," made me feel incredibly grown-up. As if Dorothy and I were initiated into a deeper realm of mystery. *The Famous Five* could keep Kirrin Island. Dorothy and I had the night.

'Good night,' Mrs. Shu,' I said.

I watched Mrs. Shu turn and head towards her bedroom where Mr. Shu with his large sad eyes was fast asleep, dreaming his hopeful dreams. Dreams in which he hadn't outlived his usefulness and spoke warmly to his children in the same way he communed with them in his heart, instead of the icy, censorious silence he gathered around him when he was awake.

In his dreams, Mr. Shu came close to understanding the great tragedy of his life was the fact his children grew to know him when he was depleted. They would never know or understand him when he was twelve, seventeen, or twenty-five and as a result, never stumble upon him at his most patient and kind.

He strove mercilessly with every tool to hand to make them better than him. They would always stand out in England and in standing out would have to stand for something. He needed them to be better than him, to never experience the backbreaking poverty and sadness of his youth. Hearing his mother speak about the bored inhabitants of palatial houses spitting on their marbled floors just to see her clean it up. Seeing his father shattered by every blow he received in the boxing ring making him excessively tender with Mr. Shu. His father, glowed with injured love, brutal and cruel in its way. Molasses thick.

That word, 'better.' If asked to explain what it meant; how he made room for it in his life, tried to accommodate it with his past, with his days to come. If asked to fully articulate what it meant without slipping into sentiment, Mr. Shu would grow flustered, and begin patting the pocket-sized calculator in his top left breast pocket as though it were a talisman of good fortune prone to bouts of wanderlust unless frequently reassured by the presence of his fingers. Mr. Shu would begin wheeling out words in a thick, guttural accent which made it next to impossible to understand what he was getting at. You, me, anyone with the best will in the world, growing impatient, compassion fatigue settling in and pulling up a chair as Mr. Shu grew more sorrowful at his inability to make himself understood.

His children, Dorothy and Stanley with their olde worlde English names running scared or penitent in his company. Preferring to stay in the kitchen with their mother and leaving him to his corrections in the front room. Days go by without them speaking, and it was a horror to him when he realised he was more at ease with his students. In dreams, Dorothy and Stanley sat close to him without fear of censure. They knew and understood him when his defining acts of kindness; the full conflation of the person he hoped to grow into took place when he hung around the main post office in Ipoh. Translating letters into English for anyone who needed him to.

With time he grew close to the young, the old, the hungry, the indifferent, the resistant, and always the words, their words, their stories, their desires, their shopping lists, spilling from his rollerball pen onto sheets of paper as he listened to them speak and wrote down what they said under the gentle susurration of three spinning ceiling fans.

Mr. Shu struggling to pin down the right words to describe the sound of the Azan in the mid-afternoon heat when the sun shone so bright, he couldn't rid himself of the suspicion if he received a cut, anywhere, he would bleed light as virulently pure and pristine as the sunlight glinting off the chrome balls toping the post and rope barrier in front of the main counter. Mr. Shu trying to get to the truth of what it felt like to be the sole witness to a wisp of smoke curling from the lit, green tip of a cheap mosquito coil. Mr. Shu striving to capture the mischievous humour of a boy who caught flies in a see-through plastic bag in order to watch them copulate and this boy needing to tell his friend Y-Y who emigrated to Kamloops B.C., all about this. How the flies moved and sometimes did not move. How he let the flies go and would spend the rest of the day drowning flying ants in the same plastic bag. This boy, compelled to tell his friend Y-Y all of this in his new language. His letter the gift of friendship and the means with which he hides his shame at being left behind.

Mr. Shu dreams and by dreaming remembers the memory of an ailing grandmother with a trembling mouth and skin the crumbly yellow of turmeric trying to correspond with a chubby, disinterested granddaughter, residing in Mares Income, Tennessee. Sitting behind the wooden horseshoe-shaped table Mr. Shu felt her words sinking into him like the punches his father received. She spoke haltingly about her morning routine, her ablutions, what she ate, listened to on the radio, the words of appeasement she uttered to keep the neighbour's dog at bay and the worry, one day soon, these words would not be enough. She mentions a sudden greening on the periphery of her vision, a grasshopper in flight, glimpsed from her front step on her way here, setting off a chain reaction so she can't help but see green, green, everywhere. She says all this in the crowded post office (a rippling line of people forming behind her) and in translating her words into English; Mr. Shu understands, the singular hope this ancient woman has is that her granddaughter, doesn't forget her. Mr. Shu writes her words down. Writes through the tears forming in his eyes, because like his father he is tender-hearted.

This had been a selfish quest, begun as ways and means to practice English so he could meet and impress a new genus of girls, radiant with sexy, Western affectations in the lazy way they chewed Bazooka Joe bubble gum and stuck their thumbs out for taxis. These girls were dangerous, suddenly in his vision like wild mushrooms sprouting every which way after days of non-stop rain. He knew these girls were going to rule the world someday. There was a part of him eager for this to happen. There was a part of him afraid for this to happen. He began paying more attention to his clothes. He stopped wearing the Baju Melayu and Sampan in public. He worked overtime in the ice factory so he could afford Western attire. Two weeks after acquiring his new garments he begins brushing his teeth with toothpaste rather than Kayu Sugi and when he walked from place to place he discovered he did so with his hands in his back pockets like he'd seen James Dean do in a movie. He copies down English words from love songs, movies, books, and magazines. However, he soon discovered he was detached from them. The words he copied lacked urgency, heft. Their function far too noticeable, predictable, like a key opening a door. No reverb to them like the sound of rain on corrugated rooftops; issuing a warning to get busy with the work of constructing a new ark.

One day on his way to work, Mr. Shu stopped by the post office to post a letter for his mother. He looked around, saw people, their gait, their teeth, their hair, the soft unglue of their mouths, heard a word reckoned with and asked to be spelled in English by the counter, and just like that, the idea was there, waiting for him.

'I can help you with that,' he announced. 'P.E.A.N.U.T.S,' he said, spelling out each letter, adding, 'I'll write it down for you.'

Now, without knowing how exactly, it has become so much more. This writing, this recording, this remembering of promises to keep not his own, yet became his, as much a part of him as the uninspired skin around his elbows or the embarrassment he feels when he watches his father rinse his bleeding mouth with saltwater and he wonders what deficiency of character, of spirit, keeps him from offering his body in his father's stead.

His battle, he suspects, is elsewhere. Not in the ring, with searing rope burns, jabs, uppercuts, counter attacks, feints, rabbit punches and fancy footwork. It's in the post office, writing down the words of strangers. In the beginning, he came during his lunch break. Now he visits before and after work.

The post office staff viewed him with distrust, another strain on their last nerve, joke with him now. Some of the male members try to pair him up with their sisters. If they're practicing they joke about him falling in love with their sister's silhouette. If they are not practicing they joke about him falling in love with their sister's cooking. Some of the female staff wonder what would happen if a woman sat at the table, writing letters in English. What would be revealed to her? What would be taken? Would she speak to them of all that she learnt?

The post office staff supplied the metal stool and table shaped like a horseshoe, tucked to the right of the main entrance. They offer Mr. Shu Kickapoo Joy Juice to combat his thirst when they see sweat beading his forehead. They touch him as they walk by. They can't help themselves.

One day a shirtless taxi driver broken into and ransacked by his anger speaks of his devotion to the singer Ella Fitzgerald. As he writes Mr. Shu realises the taxi driver is talking about Billie Holiday. Write to her and tell her I love her, the taxi driver says. I adore her music, her voice, and the flower in her hair. Send my letter to her recording company. While Mr. Shu rapidly flicks his pen up and down, and then rubs it between his palms to get the ink going, the taxi driver demands to see what the word 'love' looks like in English. His mouth forms an ugly line as he takes in the word Mr. Shu points to with the tip of his fountain pen he no longer feels guilty about stealing. So small the taxi driver says. The taxi driver offers to pay for the letter, grows angrier when Mr. Shu explains there's no charge. The taxi driver rips the letter to smithereens and walks away cursing. He meets stares with his rage, finding inspiration in the fear it inspires.

Later.

A heartsick sixteen-year-old girl calmly dictates a letter to matinee idol Rudolph Valentino even though he's been dead for years. She slips 20 Ringgit in the envelope because she knows times are hard for immigrants.

Mr. Shu writes it all down. Then he hands what he has written back. Barely having time to register the recipient heading towards the counters, where the letters will be weighed, covered with stamps before beginning their long journeys over lands and overseas.

One Saturday afternoon, sitting at the horse-shoe shaped table, with little room to move his hands due to the pile of leaflets hemming in his elbows and exhausted with trying to find the right words, trying to get to the heart of what was being said and not said, mindful of the minutes left before closing, of the increasing demands of his real job, being run ragged by a tyrannical boss with a Hollywood bad guy moustache and worn out by thoughts of his father, his mother, how much he loves them, worries he disappoints them.

Also he's frustrated, bewildered because he's never had sex. All his friends have and brag about it endlessly while he sits on the back of their motorcycles and he's stuck, sitting here, while the swirl of life goes on all around him, without him and the bad mango he ate in a hurry this morning aggravates his belly and he's beginning to feel like a spectacle, an exhibit, sitting here in the post office. Others his age, his friends, for instance, take his friends as an example, are at the beach or in distant rooms, touching, kissing, having sex, and here he is, using up his free time all the time. Writing, he's writing, gripping the pen so tightly he wonders why it doesn't shatter and it is so hot. Geckoes lie on the floor too stunned to move and only two of the three ceiling fans – the middle one out of commission going on weeks – are spinning and spinning so slowly they might as well not be spinning at all and the bad mango he wolfed down this morning feels like battery acid searing through his stomach and he's not at the beach or in a room lost in tender loving arms. There's no soft mouth yielding against his. No complicated bra strap he's engaged with because he's in the boiling hot post office and why don't these stupid, ugly people, demanding his attention, learn to write English for themselves? Or not write letters at all? Just set the person in the foreign country free, since, as far back as he can remember, not once, has he been asked to read a letter back to any of the people ordering him to write in English. Then again why would they? If anyone, in far away South Africa or Australia wrote back, wouldn't they just do so in Malay or Cantonese?

This is pointless work and the knowledge he thinks he gains useless knowledge. It won't get him any closer to those mysterious girls with their craggy voices. Come to think of it, he's beginning to suspect it does the exact opposite. Encases him in solitude like the doomed flying ants in the see-through plastic bag Y-Y spoke about. Of course, the fact of the mango. Why did he have to go and eat it in the first place? It looked rotten with fatigue like his father's face before and after a fight. His father. His mother. The heat, the beach, the spoilt mango, sweat dripping down his armpits, the pen refusing to break. The unsightly bump on his index finger caused by holding the pen for hours, a gritty itch in the middle of his ears that doesn't pack up and go when he digs his pen lid into his left ear and scrapes it about. No joy to be found there. He goes to his right ear, does the same thing with the pen lid, still no relief. His tongue, circling his dry lips, stacks of leaflets on the horseshoe table announcing the glories of sanitation, geckoes on the floor, sex, the heat, sex and only two of three ceiling fans working.

His hands are turning to fists when he looks up and there she is. Needing help with her registration forms. The blandness of her request offends him. He barely manages to suppress a groan of self-pity. Nonetheless, her voice claws through the itchy sensation percolating between his ears.

'How do I do this?' she asks with a laugh shaking up his molecules. Her laugh is a breathy exhale, the kind a dragon makes expelling gusts of steam from its snout. She is laughing at herself in a bizarre manner, as if her laughter is the conclusion to a conversation she's been having in her head for some time. He's curious, he wants that laugh for himself. He needs to hear it again.

She writes him while she studies in the United Kingdom. Her initial slew of letters filled with her replies to constantly being asked if colonial rule was so terrible. Her answers are bright like contraband and make him laugh out loud when he reads them. He likes it when she crosses out words she's spelt wrong. The sturdy line cutting across them like the restraining bar on a fairground ride keeping his body in place. He enjoys running his fingers over her handwriting, the raised scarification, evidence of the fact she presses her pen down hard upon the paper, to ensure her words don't slip away. She numbers the pages of her letters. The pages are not always from the same notebook or jotting pad, and they are not always the same size, shape, or colour, so numbering them is a great help. Mr. Shu notices she has an odd way of writing the number 8. She forgoes the necessary curvature and boldly places one circle on top of another. Her rebel eight he tells himself.

Recently she includes temporary tattoos she gets free with boxes of candy sticks and he wonders if this her way of telling him she has taken up smoking or is considering getting a tattoo. She asks if he stills goes to the post office and he begins a long letter trying to explain. He rips this letter up, and starting again, simply writes, 'You know the answer better than me.'

He writes about work. Sheets of ice the size of elevator doors and how skilful he is handling them with a metal hook. He writes about his childhood, of trying to catch guppy fish in flash puddles created by monsoons and burst pipes. He writes of outcast scorpions living behind his books.

Mr. Shu reads her letters to his parents because they love him and delight in his happiness. His father listens with swollen eyes while his mother, by the window, pretends not to be listening at all.

There are things she writes he keeps to himself. His parents know this. You and I know this. This is an old story, I give Mr. Shu to dream.

I did not know where Stanley was. He was a boy and boys are accorded more freedom to roam. Stanley however, bless his cotton socks, never struck me as the wandering type, especially at night. He was just Stanley: overgrown school-boy, frequently wind-blasted and good-natured but reserved with it, cautiously drawing on whatever sustenance remained from the love light lavished on his sister by his parents. Their regard for Dorothy exhausted them, wrung them dry so when he arrived, out of the blue, there was barely anything left. Stanley was not enraged or particularly dismayed by this, just sort of accepting, intent to get by on whatever ragged scraps of affection came his way. This gave him a certain absent-minded charm, which could be quite disarming, potentially romantically devastating if he ever learnt to weaponise it. Stanley always had this childish momentum and enthusiasm about him, clearly noticeable, when he opened up and started speaking about comics (I remember him frothing at the mouth when he noted, Darlene, from *Roseanne* had a poster of *The Endless* from *The Sandman* comic on the back of her bedroom door. While he explained who *The Endless* were Dorothy and I rolled our eyes) and Tower Cranes. Stanley adored Tower Cranes.

He was hopelessly devoted to how they moved, their staggered grace, how astute and solitary they were with their stately counterweights suspended over forever. Stanley frequently made pilgrimages to building construction sites and spent hours watching Tower Cranes. He captured them in a purple notebook he carried about with him. He drew Tower Cranes forlorn and romantic, true to life in the way a stranded glove by the roadside can be suffused with more humanity than the hand it once covered.

Stanley's drawings spread across the pages like moss and I was afraid to touch them in case they gave off heat like sheets of paper shot out of a photocopier. Once, to my great surprise,

Stanley ripped a page for me to keep. I didn't ask for it or make approving sounds when it came up. Nonetheless, Stanley must have sensed some need in me, some kinship with this particular drawing. He grew quite insistent I take it, which was rare because Stanley was always so accommodating, sorta like Penfold, from *Danger Mouse*. Stanley shoved the torn page in my hand, wouldn't listen to my mumbled objections, waved them off with gusto, edging on vehemence. I thanked him. 'There's no need to thank me,' Stanley said. He sounded angry, I remember that now. He also sounded confused by his anger. Putting away his notebook he missed the worried glance his mother and Dorothy shared. I framed the page. It's on my bedroom wall. I came this close to using it as the cover for my first album. In the end, I didn't want to share. I just didn't want to share.

Stanley had an unfortunate horse braying laugh capable of stopping traffic and he was marked with a rather curious habit of raising his hand to cover his teeth whenever he laughed as though he were ashamed of them. If memory serves, he had no reason to be. His teeth were even and clean. He inherited his mother's gap.

Stanley was bullied at school. He took this in his stride which bewildered and frustrated his tormentors. Impressed by his stoicism they tried to coerce him into their ranks with threats of ill ranging from draipsin' him up in the main hallway when he least expected it, to spitting in his hair while he waited in line for the tuck shop, his head stuck in the pages of some comic or other. When these intimidation tactics failed

Stanley's bullies went for broke, promising rare Panini stickers of football sensation Bruce Grobbelaar. Stanley politely declined their offer. He wasn't really into football, thanks. The bullies glared at him in awe and confusion as though he were as exotic and rare a creature as an owl in daylight.

'It's because you're into Rugby?' one of his bullies asked hopefully.

'Sadly no,' Stanley said, getting hit upside his head.

There was simply no revolt to him. When he told us about being asked if Bruce Lee was his dad, then being called BBC, Stanley did not appear particularly bothered. He probably wouldn't have said anything to us if Dorothy hadn't noticed his My Pet Monster rucksack was missing its right horn.

'At least they said Bruce Lee instead of Jimmy Wang Yu,' Stanley said.

'Who's that?' I asked.

'Exactly,' Stanley said.

'Is that a joke?' Dorothy asked.

'BBC?' I asked.

'British Born Chinese,' Stanley said.

'I'm going to kill them,' Dorothy said.

'I don't understand,' I said.

'Rip them limb from limb,' Dorothy said.

'I was born and raised here so I'm not fully Chinese,' Stanley said with a shrug of his shoulders.

'I still don't get it,' I said.

'I'll pulverise them,' Dorothy said, making a fist of her right hand and slamming it into the open palm of her left hand. 'Gore their eyes out and sip their blood like wine.'

'You *are* British-born Chinese though,' I said.

'Hold-up, are you telling my brother who he is?' Dorothy asked.

'No,' I said, 'I mean, wait, you were both born here, right?'

'BBC,' Stanley said.

'I'll kill them,' Dorothy said.

'They were insulting me for being Chinese even though I'm not Chinese enough for them because I wasn't born in China,' Stanley explained.

'I'll show them who we are,' Dorothy said, pushing her chin forward.

'It's fine Dorrie, really. I just wish they hadn't ripped up my comics. I doubt I'll be able to find another first issue of *Rom: SpaceKnight*, anytime soon.'

'They what?' I asked.

'Pay attention will you,' Dorothy said.

'My comics,' Stanley said, 'they were in my rucksack.'

'What about the horn?' I asked.

'I told you, they yanked it off and took it.'

'A blood bath, I'm going to give them, like you're always saying Pacific, "the whole nine yards."'

'I don't remember ever saying...'

'Dorrie, I'm fine,' Stanley said.

'...the whole nine yards, I don't remember ever saying that.'

'You are always saying stuff like that, weird war stuff,' Dorothy said.

'I am?' I asked.

'Don't worry,' Stanley said.

Stanley's voice was so reasonable, so calming, Dorothy would eventually settle down and hug her brother tightly. Their hug was so close, I was never entirely sure how either of them managed to survive it without broken bones. Dorothy, her anger, volcanic seconds ago, inert and docile now, so much so it felt like something I had imagined, appropriated to fuel my middling sense of outrage.

As was generally the case when all three of us were together, we were in their kitchen. I didn't know or think to ask where their parents were. Stanley's My Pet Monster rucksack was lying face-up on the kitchen table, morbidly still like a body on a mortuary slab. Cotton stuffing leaked out the tear where the right horn had been.

'Who is Jimmy Wang Yu?' I asked.

I remember Stanley.

Women would glance at him and decide there wasn't particularly much going on behind the brown eyes staring back at them in whatever poorly lit pub they happened to be sitting in. These women would never know, most mornings, come rain or shine, he was a singing man, glorious in the disrepair of his voice. I believed Stanley was at his most beautiful with his head buried in one of his notebooks. There was a simple splendour in how detached he was from everything around him when he drew. It was precious to me, witnessing this, because it didn't demand my presence, didn't need me to comment on it, was as complete a vision onto itself as the sky at dusk. I had no trouble believing this was Stanley at his most beautiful. Of course, I was wrong. Did I mention, I might have forgotten to say, he was a singing man.

The women watching Stanley sip his beer, nursing it slowly, trying to work up an appetite for its coterie of sputtering bubbles, holding back a crunchy burp as he politely placed the pint-glass back on the beer coaster, understood that Stanley, had an unabashed innocence about him. He was of that type. If he owned a bicycle, bet your life this bicycle would have a name like Bandit or Silver and there was more than a good chance he would stick a magpie's feather somewhere on the bicycle to facilitate its powers of flight. Stanley was always a boy growing up to be a dreamy man with his sight set somewhere over the horizon.

I remember wondering where he was that night. Was he asleep or roaming streets? A happy exile searching for T Cranes in the dark. There was no way standing in his hallway as Dorothy reached for a jacket I could have guessed how slowly he would undress me the first and only time we made love. How in the kerfuffle and blunder of our bodies colliding and us giggling past the panic he would suddenly stop and begin putting on my clothes.

There were rips and rends in my tights because Stanley wasn't careful pulling them on, denier fibre thickness in the upper 60s, be dammed. Stanley put my Fido Dido T-shirt on back-to-front which meant Fido's face was hidden from me which was probably for the best because no way on God's good green could I have taken Fido's brand of insouciance just then. My orange box pleated skirt looked cartoon sluttish on Stanley, like Bugs Bunny in drag. It didn't help the dress was kitty printed and Stanley's erection was making one of the kitten's eyes appear boss-eyed which by rights should have bled desire clean out of me but didn't. Stanley looked outlandish but also incredibly sexy. I took immense pleasure looking at him and contemplating the glide of his body under the fluttery pressure of my clothes. With my clothes on him, Stanley smelled a little like me, like he raided my bathroom and applied my Palmer's cocoa butter cream to his arms, legs, chest, the back of his knees. When we kissed, he tasted gritty like rain water caught in the hollow of a tyre swing.

Without giving it much thought, I gently pulled away from Stanley. I began putting on his clothes. Stanley's clothes were scattered all over my bed and bedroom floor like pieces from a shipwreck. I gathered them up. I took a sniff of his shirt, scrunching my eyes at the oniony smell. Stanley burst out laughing. He made no attempt to hide his teeth.

His boxers, damp with pre-cum, I slipped on, after turning them inside out. His rip curl 'Original Case' baseball cap I placed on my head, with the bill facing the back. His black trousers kept sliding down my hips, so I had to cinch it tighter with his belt, sticking the prong in the belt's very last hole. I buttoned up his shirt while Stanley fussed with my red lace, neck choker like it was alien technology. Against Stanley's skin, lighter than mine, it looked less like blood and more like festive wrapping. Once it was on his neck, Stanley began undressing me like I was wrapped in kite string. Stanley took off his/my cap and threw it across the room with the tyrannical zeal of a teenage Zeus hurling a lightning bolt. Stanley grew hesitant with my hair, each lock, I'm guessing, as unknowable to him as a snake on the head of the Medusa. With a tilt of my hips, I let Stanley know I wasn't that delicate. Stanley's eyebrows were not at all boomerang-shaped and yet, they still appeared capable of sailing off his forehead when he ran his fingers through my hair, dislodging the pencil keeping my dreads up. Stanley undid the buttons on my/his shirt while I pulled down his/my orange pleated skirt. I kissed Stanley's eyes shut. I kissed the taut skin beneath the red lace neck choker I bought from a bread-faced girl down Camden sides with bulky Ankh earrings dangling from each ear and smoky kohl around her eyes.

I was kissing Stanley and Stanley was kissing me when I flashed on the memory of a ghostly impression behind a high curtained window. Nestled within this memory I was also thinking about the dishes piled up in the sink and since I cooked, would Stanley do the dishes or would I wind up doing them? I was also thinking, find it find it. Your sister left a star in my head years ago, find it find it. There were a cluster of blackheads on Stanley's nose. With my fingers I could destroy each and every one, rain down death from above by squeezing them. I could imagine the satisfying pop of their annihilation ringing in my ears, but Stanley, with some instinct for their self-preservation, moved in a way that made me realise my trusty Fido Dido T-shirt was getting all stretched out due to his husky frame and would have to be relegated to nightwear. I left the blackheads alone. I reached for the T-shirt.

Stanley, kissing me, his tongue going round and round at

speed like a washing machine in its spin cycle began plucking away at his/my belt buckle. While using new runs in his/my tights as pathways for my fingers, thumbs, and butterfly kisses, I heard music.

It was.

I swear.

Hand on heart.

Believe me.

Please.

I swear.

Music.

All the songs I taped for Dorothy years ago. Circling us like wraiths. I heard Leonard Cohen gloat about having a pussy in the kitchen and a panther in the yard as Stanley pinioned my wrists against the headboard. 'Marion's Declaration of Love' from the soundtrack for the film *Wings of Desire* was burbling in my bloodstream when I arched my back and witnessed Stanley's face contort in a way that made me want to laugh. I bit my lower lip but laughter escaped and ran free while Stanley (with patient dexterity that felt like payback) prodded and circled my belly button with a tongue intent on breaking skin.

At times Stanley's rhythm was off; probably because he lost track of me, and suddenly saw and felt himself entwined with one of the masked superheroines in the comics he still read. After two or more nibs on his ears, Stanley returns to me. He surrenders to a deeper melody and I wonder if Stanley is hearing the same music I'm hearing. Is there a chance of such a thing being possible? Could he be as riled up as I am by the pensive drum beat in 'Heart and Soul' by Joy Division? Is he perturbed by the stark choice Ian Curtis offers between the heart and the soul and one having to burn?

The dishes are still waiting in the sink when I bury my elbows deeper into the mattress for ballast and the pencil which held my dreads in place rolls off the bed. Stanley, unaware of the pencil's bid at martyrdom kisses the lines and skin tags on my neck like he is trying to erase them. When I kiss Stanley, I slide my tongue across the gap in his teeth. Stanley tries to speak. I lodge my thumb in his mouth. I press down on his tongue. I use the slobber from his interior to trace the outline of a heart on my chest. For Stanley, gasping under me, his eyes watering, it might well have looked, like a star.

Lifting the shiny condom wrapper from the floor, and telling myself it looked like a stamp, a torn postage stamp, I spot the pencil near the foot of my bed. I pick it up. Stanley, naked as the day he was born, watches the pencil disappear under my dreads.

Dorothy called me three days ago. Heaven knows how she got my number. She told me Stanley was dead. Killed instantly when he walked in front of a bus. He stepped off the pavement into a sort of eternity. She invited me to the funeral and I...I...I... I...

Stanley like his father was probably fast asleep.

'What are you thinking about?' Dorothy wanted to know as we made our way to the front door.

'Your father and Stanley,' I said, still running on plonker time for real.

'Nasty business,' Dorothy said.

'Not like that, just what they might be doing.'

'You think too much,' Dorothy said.

'I don't think so,' I said.

'Is that a joke?' Dorothy asked, picking up her house keys from inside a fluffy slipper next to its burgundy twin.

'That's ever a strange place to keep keys,' I said.

'Strange as some but not as strange as others,' Dorothy replied.

'You listen, you actually listen,' I said.

'Snoring and farting,' Dorothy said with a faraway grin.

'Pardon?' I said.

'Stanley and Dad,' Dorothy said, 'farting and snoring, that's what they're doing.'

Dorothy and I leave her house. The moon, like the stars, is nowhere to be found. The fresh air does something to us. We begin giggling uncontrollably. The sound we make echoes and reverberates through us, peeling back another layer of night revealing us walking and giggling. When we stop, we wipe tears from our eyes.

It was a warm and balmy night; Dorothy didn't need a jacket. She'd grabbed one anyway, an emerald green jean jacket, which went rather well with what she was wearing, rounded everything off in a pleasing way. Dorothy stood close to me; it was as though she vibrated, gave off a slight electric charge which made the hair on the back of my neck stand on end. She kept re-adjusting the purple hibiscus in her hair like she was worried it would fall off. Dints of yellow light from streetlamps we walked under lit up its stamen and pistil in mouth-watering ways.

Dorothy and I walked. We do not speak to each other. Our giggling fit using up our need and capacity for words. We reach the end of her road. My eyes kept drifting down to glance at my feet then gazing hungrily at the purple hibiscus in Dorothy's hair. Down to my feet again, and up again, my sight, momentarily harangued by the low-pressure sodium glare of a streetlamp. The streetlamp's light was fuzzily iridescent. A tattered strand from a spider's web clung to the bulb. This image sunk deep inside me with no easy explanation as to why it made me so feel cherished.

Dorothy and I are standing in front of a closed hair salon called Hair Today Gone Tomorrow. Its grey shutters resolutely pulled down as though guarding the shop's innards against the apocalypse. Dorothy and I are waiting for a bus. I turn and look into the hairdressers. By narrowing my eyes and angling my head upwards I'm just about able to see through the thin metallic slats blanketing the shop. I see styling chairs. I see free-standing MDF shelves filled with bottles of all shapes and sizes. Right at the back is a large, imposing mirror.

Dorothy and I are sitting on a bus. The N41 heading for Archway proper. Before it arrives there it will have to pass through Black Boy Lane, a stretch of road I knew intimately. It being part of my paper-round route not so long ago.

All this to say, I remembered leaving my old bedroom with its warm duvet. Having to make sure I did not trip over Mastermind, so much younger then and always pretending to be asleep on the ninth stair as I staggered bleary-eyed and mealy-mouthed towards the front door. The roaring blast of cold air hitting me in the face doing next to nothing to rouse me from my slumberous state. I was listening to my Walkman. The opening theme for *The Mysterious Cities of Gold* I recorded off TV, sounding far too loud and knocking my thoughts aside as easily as Godzilla toppled buildings. I turned the volume down and after a few more steps, I quietly sang along. '*Children of the sun/see your time as just begun/ searching for your way/to adventures every day.*' Then the chorus, that wondrous soaring chorus kicked in, making me close my eyes, even though the dangers of stepping in dog shit were real. Of being kidnapped was real. Of being dazzled by parallelograms of light with no detectable origin, was real. I closed my eyes anyway. Inoculated against calamity because I had my music with me.

By the time I opened my eyes I had successfully made it to the newsagents at the bottom of my street. Ta-dah. I rang the bell I always ring. I pressed the stop button on my Walkman. The voices in my ears stop. I take off my headphones and let them dangle round my neck. The galvanised steel security shutter in front of me ascends with a metallic whirring sound like a ship dropping anchor. I push the glass door open. Warm air hits me in the face like I said something horrible about its mum.

After getting the newspapers from the newsagent, every step I take is weighed down due to the shifting weight of the high-visibility yellow bag slung across my right shoulder like an old school bandolier. Rocking from side to side and trying to maintain my balance I see swards of grass peppered with frost twinkling away in the early light. I smiled to myself, happy to be alive to observe such a thing.

I'm saying I saw myself reading *Peanuts* cartoon strips on the back page of the *Daily Mail* under a sky rippling with a fantastic lineage of purple and pinks and it was super easy for me to believe the sky was mine entirely, at least for a little while, since, as far as I could tell, I was the only person around.

I was thirteen years old, moving through a world still dreaming its dreams. And when the Ever Ready batteries in my Walkman fizzled out; under my breath, into the cold air shaping and caressing my words into near-perfect facsimiles of the speech bubbles rising from Charlie Brown's mouth in the strip I just read, I start singing. I sing whatever songs pop into my head from what I heard on the radio or seen performed on *The Chart Show* or *Top of the Pops*. I begin making up my own songs. As I sang the world, and all the things in it seemed interested in me. Not only interested, invested in my wellbeing.

This memory of me as a papergirl is running through my head while Dorothy and I sat on the bus and I want to relay something about this to her. The mystique of being awake when nearly everyone I knew was fast asleep. The sheer exhaustion of the work, especially on Sundays with all the extra entertainment supplements swelling up the paper bag and adding extra drag to my feet as I panted and sweated my way up and down endless flights of dimly lit council estate stairs.

Trying my best not to be alarmed when I saw graffiti which read: 'Cursed Hebona For Free,' 'Bentfin Bommer Girls for Life,' and 'Tragic Roundabout,' scrawled on crumbling walls streaked with the vinegary whiff of human pee.

I also wanted to explain to Dorothy how it was in the squat newsagent. The factory vinyl flooring smelling of unwashed feet and the distinguished owners, the podgy husband in Nazarene sandals and his slightly less podgy wife, softened by sleep. Every one of their pores secreting the wanton vulnerability of the somnambulist making me a bit suspicious of them and unable or just unwilling to fully comprehend the twilight language floating from the not-so-podgy wife's lips until I respond by giving her a pencil from the shelf behind me.

The not-so-podgy wife ignores my staring at the red kumkum dot on her forehead. She takes the pencil and writes on the air. Arabesque flourishes, diagonal slashes, curvilinear shapes. She does this for a while, the not-so-podgy wife, scribbling on the air, and then she smiles to herself, remembering what it is she's supposed to be doing. The not-so- podgy wife shuffles past me and writes down the addresses of houses I'm delivering to on the stack of newspapers piled up on the ice-cream fridge, expelling a frail ostinato, in stark contrast to the sonorous, intestinal hum of the large refrigeration unit keeping bottles and cans of alcohol cool and appealing to the eye.

'Dorothy,' I would say, 'While the not-so-podgy wife wrote addresses down her podgy for real husband would mention any mistakes I made the previous day. He sounded agitated right up to the point a yawn swallowed his words, robbing them of their urgency. I shrugged my shoulders in the face of his appeal for greater care while chomping on a Marathon. The price for the Marathon would be deducted from my wages and already I'm regretting it. The sticky caramel congealing in my stomach and making me feel ill. I saw the headline flash before my eyes, "Greedy girl wolfs down so-so chocolate bar, lives long enough to regret it."

'Dorothy,' I would add, leaning in close with a Guy Fawkes whisper, 'I used to work these very streets, delivering newspapers. I had a job. I was a papergirl. I used to wonder about the people sleeping behind the doors I delivered papers to. I used to wonder about the shape their heads left on their pillows, how these people encountered their loneliness, how their hands cradled their coffee cups and sometimes I was bad, naughty. I stole bottles of orange juice left on doorsteps by the milkman. I guzzled them down quick. All proud of myself for doing something wrong and getting away with it.'

'Dorothy,' I would add cheerfully, 'I was young and already tricky with nostalgia for the moment I was living through.'

Dorothy and I are sitting on the top deck, which, apart from the two of us, is completely empty. The windows have strange hieroglyphics and migrating dicks in various states of tumescence etched on them. The back seats hum with the greasy smell of fried chicken. The strained occultism in the air forces me to hold my tongue. Dorothy and I do not move. We are quiet, close to reverent. The avocado head-shaped bus driver barely registering on our radar, although I have to say, I enjoyed the disinterest with which he gave me my change once I paid for my ticket. Dorothy flashed her monthly travel card with all the confidence and speed of an F.B.I. agent and I, having no idea where we were going, paid for the journey's end.

The bus driver, like Charon, who has seen and heard it all, gave me my change without bothering to look at me like black girls in billowy white shirts were all the rage. Even at this ungodly hour.

Dorothy was sitting near the window caught up in her thoughts. Her freckles, luminescent like train tracks at night.

'Where are we going? I asked.

Dorothy doesn't answer. I wasn't sure she'd heard me. I tried again. Sounding as whiny as before.

Dorothy says.

'We're here.'

'Here is where? I asked, standing up.

We leave the bus; it glides from us quickly, not particularly big on goodbyes this one. I watched it turn with sinewy ease into Green Lanes. The bus sails past a shop called Nomad, trading in travel equipment. Tents, camouflage fatigues, malaria kits, canteens. Next to Nomad, its façade lovingly garnished with the foamy yellow hue of a Lucozade bottle filled with piss, a McDonald's.

The temperature has dropped. A cold breeze makes me tuck my chin down and lift my shoulders up as if I'm adamant about transforming myself into a living, breathing question mark. Duckett's Common lours behind us. There is a bicycle, painted white, padlocked to the metal fence circling the Common. There are red votive candles in front of the bicycle. Dorothy and I cross the road.

We stroll past Turnpike Lane tube station, all locked up. In a few hours, it will have a bellyache of people wriggling about in front of it. Dorothy and I hustle down a side street at speed which leaves me disorientated. I hear birds singing, mistaking the dazzle of neon for the break of day.

The side street we're on twists and shifts into another street then another. I step on something and it sounds like I'm stepping on human teeth. I cringe before glancing down. All I've done is step on sprinkles of rock salt.

Dorothy is walking faster. I'm having difficulty keeping up with her. We're heading towards a street named something I can't recall three seconds after reading its name on a sign. I hear a sound cut through the night, a high-pitched beeping like a barcode being read by a shop, till scanner. I pick up the pace like it's a five-pound note I've spotted on the pavement and the sound my footsteps make echoing off house fronts comes close to rattling loose the last of my confidence.

A cat darts under a car. As it slips from view I notice it's the perfect opposite of Mastermind. A white cat with paws that looked like it had stepped in a puddle of black paint.

Dorothy stands in front of a semi-detached house with a yellow door. I nearly crash into her. Dorothy pats down her emerald green jean jacket like she's searching for keys. She cautiously runs her hands over her legs to get rid of any lint she might have picked up on the bus.

'How do I look?'

'Amazing,' I said, slightly taken aback by how exhausted my voice sounds.

'I hope so,' Dorothy replied.

Dorothy fusses with the purple hibiscus in her hair. All the way here it was perfectly aligned with her beauty, augmenting it, widening its scope. Due to her tweaking, it's slightly askew. On a perilous lean like the celebrated Tower of Pisa.

I move in. My breathing curled in on itself like a sleeping sea horse as I slowly reach out and adjust the flower in Dorothy's hair.

'There,' I said, beaming with pride, 'better.'

'Thanks,' Dorothy said.

My blood was throbbing loudly in the hand I just used, throbbing loudly in my ears and I wanted to turn and run. Run home. I wanted my mum. I wanted Mastermind and some curious quality of his quaint starvation. I remained rooted to the spot with an imbecile's pride in how stunning Dorothy looked. Stupefied by how in some small way I contributed to her immaculate beauty by righting the flower in her hair.

Dorothy makes her way towards the house with the yellow door. When she rings the bell I see welts and tears in the door's paintwork. The doorbell emits a death rattle gurgle making it clear its cache of batteries were on their last legs and a new batch would have to be purchased from Dixons, as soon as possible.

The door did not open. Dorothy, tentatively, knocked on the ground floor window.

The door opened.

'Ha, you.'

A loud voice belonging to a tall boy with an extremely round face. At a push, he was three, possibly four years older than us.

'Come in, come on in,' he said, with the easy warmth of a

game show host. He bowed deeply before pivoting to his left to let us by. These motions, the deep bow, the tilt to his left, were far too extravagant and he chuckled bitterly to himself while making them. He slammed the door shut behind us.

The spacious hallway smelt of dog, hoary wet dog. The hallway carpet was a strange colour like the burnished underside of a crab. There was a series of interlocking cable trunking creeping along the wall with no visible baseboard electrical outlet or telephone socket. On the very same wall, closer to where I stood, was an oak framed picture of a seated Bedouin with a faraway look in his rheumy eyes. The sky-blue scarf wrapped around his neck appeared to be strangling him which had the effect of making the faraway look in the Bedouin's eyes him contemplating the other side of eternity.

There were stairs in front of me floating into darkness which appeared layered with more darkness. At the foot of the stairs, a chipped, toffee-coloured dog bowl, filled with water. The bowl was peppered with bird droppings which put the quease on me something quick. I looked closer and realised it wasn't bird droppings but moths. There were so many, it looked like they were trying to reconstitute themselves into a grey pelt. During their celestial orientation, something fatal had occurred to knock these moths off course. Instead of the moon, street lamps, a billowing white duvet on a clothesline, these moths had been seduced by a decoy eye. I nearly fell to my knees to rescue them. If not for the fact the water appeared toxic, I would have saved them if I could.

On the opposite side of the wall, directly in front of the

framed picture of the meditating Bedouin was a black and white poster. The poster showed a policeman in full battle regalia leaning down to talk to a little girl. Under the girl's feet, the declaration: "Mum Told Me Never to Talk to Bastards."

I was staring at the poster but really I was in danger of becoming ensorcelled by the cable trunking which appeared to be pulsing in synch with the rise and fall of moth wings in the dog bowl.

'Look who's here,' the tall boy announced cheerfully, as he led us into the front room. The self-same room with the window Dorothy knocked on earlier, although I could have sworn, the window had curtains, not blinds.

'Oh, hi Dorothy.'

The owner of this voice rose from a sofa covered with heaps of what appeared to be flesh-coloured blankets. It was hot in the front room, the central heating going full tilt. I couldn't see how anyone could take being covered with so many blankets in a room close to liquefying. The owner of the voice had a Tintin quiff, which usually had me thinking of adventure; Tintin on a motorcycle with Snowy in its sidecar. This time round it made me slightly uneasy, like instead of being hair, it was a bony protrusion, a horn of some sort.

As the shape rose from the sofa sweat trickled down my forehead. Free of blankets he was about medium height with powerful, stumpy legs, like Super Mario. He also had a flat as flat can be nose. I had to squint to make out nostrils and even then they appeared somewhat occasional. A spit-slick toothpick dangled from the right hinge of his mouth. It looked sharp. I worried he would cause himself a mischief with it. Not only himself.

Eczema. There was eczema on his neck, the tips of his ears, around his mouth, all raw and scalding red like a Turkey's neckpiece. Looking at him made me feel itchy and in serious need of a bath. I admit this might have had something to do with the cloying smell of wet dog clinging to everything in the room. I found myself searching for where the dog might be as Dorothy opened her arms to hug Toothpick Boy. He was wearing a blue frock coat which lent him the appearance of a diminutive Hessian soldier. Like his confederate, he was older than us. As he made his way towards Dorothy's hug I heard clanking. I glanced down. There were empty beer cans strewn in front of the sofa.

The round-faced, tall boy who opened the front door for us was standing next to me. He smelled swampy, like spoilt malt loaf. He had on a black Nehru jacket. As he watched Dorothy hug his friend, I heard him chuckle.

After their hug, guy with toothpick turned, stared at me.

'Who's this when she's not at home?'

Dorothy, right arm curled round his waist, answered.

'Pacific, 'member I told you about her?'

'Ahhhhh the Pacific Monster,' the Tall One said shuffling past me and heading towards a ruby red chair that looked far too small for him. Beer cans rattled ominously in his wake.

'Who now?' Toothpick asked.

'Pacific,' the Tall One and Dorothy said together.

'I mentioned her, told you I was bringing her,' Dorothy

continued patiently.

'She doesn't look at all like you made her sound,' Toothpick replied.

'Yes she does,' Dorothy said.

'I'm Pacific,' I said loudly to authenticate my existence beyond the anecdotal.

'So you are,' the Tall One said with a chuckle.

Toothpick extended his right hand. Reaching for it, I heard him say. 'I'm Oberon Rifle and him, ha, that reprobate over there is Weir, Weir Miller,' he said, turning his head to where his tall friend sat with his spindly knees drawn up to his chest.

'Nice to meet you,' I managed to say once my hand was released.

'Don't forget to say hello to the reprobate,' Oberon suggested.

'Hello Reprobate,' I said.

'How about you take a powder and sit next to me,' Weir asked, enthusiastically patting the tiny space next to him. Not wanting to appear rude I avoided the empty beer cans as best I could and sat down. It was a tight squeeze. As soon as I sat down I sprang up with a yelp because I heard a sharp squeak. Weir chuckled. Dorothy and Oberon laughed as Weir threw the bone-shaped soft toy I sat on behind him.

'Sorry about that,' Weir said with a chuckle.

'No problem,' I said, smiling idiotically.

'What I tell you? Reprobate.'

'I prefer rapscallion.'

'How about dick splash?'

'What?'

'You heard me.'

'Your mum.'

'My mum?' Oberon said pointing to himself.

'Yeah.'

'Why'cha say that again?'

'Your mum.'

'And what exactly does dear ole Mum have to do with the price of milk?'

'Fucked her.'

'You did?'

'Yeah.'

'Charming,' Oberon said.

Oberon sat down on the sofa. Dorothy sat on his lap. They were both, Oberon and Dorothy, sitting on the sofa whose colour I could not fully discern or describe with any degree of accuracy which wouldn't make me out a liar. The two boys were beaming at each other.

I took a deep breath and slowly took in the room. The wood chips walls were painted grey. There were badly colourised framed photographs on the mantle above the fireplace. The fireplace was boarded up with cement. The framed pictures on the mantel were of a nuclear family standing in front of a lake. I could not tell which of the grinning boys in the pictures was Weir or Oberon. There was a mother, a father and two boys, one of which wore an eyepatch. There was also a girl, sullen, arms folded in front of her chest. She was standing slightly apart from everyone else. Staring angrily into the camera like she wanted to smash it to bits.

I did not sit down right away. My standing felt appropriate, in collusion with the atmosphere in the room which appeared to be crying out for a witness. Someone to stand apart, like the girl in the pictures did. I continued scanning the room. I saw a brown, combination lock, leather briefcase leaning against the hind legs of the stainless-steel table in front of me. There was a kitchen knife buried in the suitcase. On the table were about ten, no, five, six, eleven, wait a minute, ten, yeah, ten British Telecom telephone cards spread out like an open fan. There were a handful of chocolate gold coins on top of a *TV Times* magazine with a picture of Alan Titchmarsh caught full smug on the front cover. There was also a smaller picture of Ainsley Harriott holding a spatula and the sentence: 'Ainsley's Big Cock Out,' in bubble font lettering above the picture. Someone had terraformed the second 'O' in 'Cook' into a 'C' with Tipex.

Where was the dog? The dog. Where was it?

'Where are my manners?' Oberon asked, slapping the right side of his face viciously. 'Would any of you ladies care for a drink? I'm more than a hundred percent convinced Weir sitting pretty over there would be more than happy to get you one. If he isn't too tired after making love to my dad. Sorry, my mum. Isn't that right dear, not too tired are you?'

Weir chuckled.

'No thanks,' Dorothy offered brightly, 'we're good.'

'Not too good I hope,' Weir said with a chuckle.

Dorothy giggled. She was sitting on Oberon's lap and she giggled. She was trying to pat down his quiff, which looked sharp enough to draw blood.

The light in the room came from a naked light bulb. It was too bright, a facsimile moon, too big and obvious for the room. I did not like being here. I did not like seeing the beer cans. I did not like the solidity of the knife. I did not like the blankets lying in insensate heaps on the floor. I did not like the fact the pictures on the mantel, all five of them, revealed the same scene. I did not like seeing Dorothy sitting on Oberon's lap. I did not like noting the gilded edge of a picture frame Oberon heel kicked under the sofa when he noticed me staring at it. I did not like Weir watching me watch Dorothy patting down Oberon's quiff.

'Why don't you sit down?' Weir asked.

'Yeah,' Dorothy said.

'Sit!' Oberon commanded.

I plopped myself down on the chair's right armrest. I glanced up at the ceiling. Then I looked round the room again.

In a right corner nook a television. Had it always been there? How had I missed it? The television was on. The volume on mute. The icon for the mute symbol floated across the screen like a lazy mosquito. I tried to discern a pattern in its tiny moves. There wasn't one. The mute symbol was glow-in-the-dark green. We four stared at the screen. I suppose the mute symbol resonated with me seeing as I went on to use it as the cover for my first album: *Scheerer's Sprites*.

On the screen, a knife thrower wearing a blindfold threw knives at a woman. The woman was shackled to a door. Every time a knife hit the door, there was a tight close-up of the woman's mouth opening unhurried and assured as though she were taking a bite out of an apple. The man, tuxedoed up to the nines threw twelve knives in rapid succession. One knife tore open the woman's right thigh. Blood seeped from the wound as the woman's mouth slowly opened. The scene abruptly changes to an overhead shot of an indoor swimming pool filled with shopping trolleys, satellite dishes, fridges, wheelie-bins, washing machines, microwaves. These items writhed in ecstasy as whatever lived beneath them threatened to break the surface.

I was sitting on the edge of the ruby red chair's armrest. My hands balled into fists against my chest. I felt the chair move, wobble ever so slightly, as Weir reached down, groping for something. His right hand came up with a bulky remote control wrapped in plastic. The plastic covering was sticky like it'd been dipped in Benylin cough syrup. There were wisps of dog hair stuck to its sides. Weir pointed the control at the TV screen but the TV was at an angle and to aim at it properly, without breaking his wrist, Weir had to lean forward and he nearly fell out of his chair. The batteries in the remote must have been dead because nothing happened. I heard Weir chuckle to himself.

The swimming pool was gone, replaced by an empty room with a baby in nappies crawling across the floor. Behind the baby was an owl using its talons to tear a mole to pieces. I say it was a mole. It was a shredded tarp of black skin glistening with guts. It was a mole. A booted foot emerged and tenderly nudged the baby towards the owl.

'What next-level freaky-deaky shenanigans is this?' Dorothy asked, sounding refreshingly like the Dorothy of old.

'Supposed to be *Prime Cut*,' Weir said.

'Starring Sissy Spacek,' Oberon said.

'A young Sissy Spacek,' Weir said wolfishly.

'They must have changed the program,' Oberon said.

'I was looking forward to seeing Sissy Spacek,' Weir said.

'You sure it wasn't Lee Marvin?' Oberon asked, 'he's in the film.'

'Redheads all the way,' Weir said with a chuckle.

I glanced at Dorothy. She looked back at me, with no expression. I looked down at the table, the phone cards. The phone cards were now neatly piled on top of each other and there seemed to be more chocolate gold coins than I remembered seeing on the cover of the *TV Times* magazine.

Oberon shoved Dorothy off his lap. He stood up like a man on a mission. He strolled over to the television and switched it off. I watched all the light in the television screen collapse into one small dot.

When Oberon sat down on the sofa, he was all by himself. Dorothy had moved. She was now sitting on Weir's lap. The purple hibiscus in her hair looked beleaguered, in serious need of water. It didn't smell too great either and I thought I saw a halo of flies buzzing around it.

'I'm so glad you're here Dorothy and I'm over the moon you saw fit to bring such a delightful friend,' Oberon said.

He was glaring at me. He added, 'I like your haircut. It's a man's haircut. Like Diana Ross's in the black version of *The Wizard of OZ, The Wiz*. You ever see that film?'

'No,' I said.

'I'm telling you. Your haircut is exactly the same, it's like the haircut Diana Ross wore in the film is sitting in front of me,' Oberon said.

'Hello haircut,' Weir said with a chuckle.

Dorothy rested her head on my left shoulder and sighed. My heart started pounding as though preparing itself for a sequence of backflips. I felt a jolt of electricity shoot through my body with enough power to resurrect the lacklustre remote control, doorbell and expiring moths in the chipped, toffee-coloured dog bowl.

'Now, now, none of that, I'm the jealous type,' Oberon said, taking the toothpick from his mouth and flicking it towards Dorothy. Weir, much to my surprise managed to catch it. The toothpick was in his hand for a brief second. Then Weir placed it in his mouth.

Dorothy's head remained on my shoulder. I stayed still. I was subject to gravity as much as anyone else, but believe me when I say it felt like I was flying through space, my own body circling the rings of Saturn, with all manner of space dust and ice particles congregating within the fleshy declivity of my belly button. Oberon winked at me. And gravity returned, and Dorothy and I were not an aspect of theophany, despite the fact her head must have looked like it was growing out of my left shoulder and the heat in the room made our skin shine.

Oberon had taken a lighter from his trouser pocket and was lighting up a cigarette clenched between his pursed lips. The dried skin orbiting his lips looked irate. He stared at Dorothy. He continued staring as wobbly streaks of smoke rose in front of his face. Dorothy eyes were closed. I knew this. It's a funny thing, but I knew her eyes were closed by how serene and calm her head felt on my shoulder, which meant she did not, could not, stare back. I did though, I met his stare. I heard Weir chuckle as he manoeuvred Dorothy's head from me and kissed her on the mouth. When they stopped kissing Dorothy had the toothpick in her mouth.

'Let's go for a drive,' Oberon suggested.

'Sounds good,' Weir said.

'Getting a tad stuffy in here,' Oberon replied, looking right at me.

'A drive would be nice,' Dorothy proclaimed, the toothpick gripped in the right corner of her mouth.

'Where are we going?' I asked.

'You deaf?' Dorothy said impatiently, 'a drive.'

'In the perv-mobile,' Weir said with a chuckle.

'What?' I said.

'We're wasting time,' Oberon said standing up, 'hand me the bloody keys.'

Weir chuckled as he reached into his Nehru jacket pocket and flung a set of keys at Oberon.

'Let's get going,' Oberon said, catching the keys easily. I stood up. I heard a dog bark a warning. It sounded like it came from inside the room.

'You hear that?' I said.

'Hear what?' Dorothy asked.

'A dog, a dog barking,' I replied breathlessly.

'Que signifie le chien?' Weir said from his chair.

'Typical. One kiss and lover man starts speaking French,' Oberon said.

'The language of romance,' Weir said with a chuckle.

'Wait, what?' I said.

'I didn't hear a dog,' Dorothy said, knuckling a yawn.

'Neither did I,' Oberon replied, 'and there's no point hanging round wasting God's good air.'

'Dog or no dog,' Dorothy chimed in.

'I'm sure I heard a dog,' I said.

'It's all in your head,' Dorothy said, standing up.

'Or in your hair,' Weir said, getting to his feet.

'Is that a joke?' Dorothy asked.

'Do I fucking look like I'm joking?' Weir said with a chuckle.

I kept looking. Trying to locate the source of the bark. I was still searching when I sat in the car, in the back with Dorothy. The car was brown and wouldn't look out of place in a rain-soaked episode of *Taggart*.

The car was going fast. Way too fast. It felt like it was levitating above the road. I closed my eyes. Opened them. Oberon was driving, although, for a second there, it looked like Weir was driving. I winded down my window to let some fresh air in. I stared out my window at the world rushing by. The road we were on was empty, free of vehicles, free of people. Eerily silent, eerily peaceful, eerily prescient with doom waiting patiently for us at the next roundabout. As we drove nobody said anything, although, every now and then I heard Weir chuckle as he drove, no, wait, Oberon was driving.

We drove through the night. I must have been really tired because I dozed and had a fleeting dream in which I played an arcade machine made of human skin. The arcade stick, a yellowing femur, creaking and splintering when I took hold of it. The game was a run and jump game, and the smudgy character I controlled jumped over piles of books and threw books at winged enemies, more teeth than face. As I progressed through the level, I knew the end-of-level boss would be Dad and his weak spots, his wrists, his ankles. In most dreams I had about my father, he was always leaving a room as I entered it. In this dream, so unlike all the others, I was running and jumping through the level to do battle with him. My energy bar, the chemically enhanced yellow of a yellow jelly bean, was low. I had taken risks, make foolish mistakes, but I knew, after a few more obstacles, Dad.

I woke to the sound of laughter. Dorothy laughing. When I turned to look at her, there was no indication she'd laughed at all. I heard Oberon and Weir whispering to each other. I shuffled forward in my seat to pick up what they were saying. Weir, who was now driving twisted round and smiled at me.

'Eyes on the road Romeo,' Oberon said.

'Yeah-yeah,' Weir muttered, still smiling at me with the spit moistened toothpick, weaving about his mouth like the proboscis of an insect. He continued staring for a worrying length of time before returning his attention to the road. He chuckled. Hold on, wasn't the toothpick in Dorothy's mouth?

'I must have fallen asleep,' I said.

'Did you?' Dorothy asked.

'What time is it?' I asked.

'Earlier than late,' Dorothy replied.

The purple hibiscus in her hair looked like it was caught up in the process of gaining a new respiratory system, one laced with rust. My window which I opened was closed. There was sweat on my forehead and sweat under my armpits. I should never have worn a waistcoat in a billion years. I did not dare take it off. The more clothing I had on, the more protected I felt.

The dream was fading. I tried to focus on what the character I controlled in the dream was. Human or beast, masonry nail, skateboard or submarine. I couldn't figure. It felt important to know what my avatar had been, but the dream, its contours, were already beyond reach.

'Where are we going?' I asked with a dry taste in my mouth like I'd been sucking on burnt matches. Asking this question stopped me from lingering on the dream, and instead anchored me to the present moment like the dot in an exclamation mark.

'On a drive,' Dorothy said, the toothpick suddenly reappearing in her mouth.

'Know once we get there, sleepyhead,' Oberon said, attempting to sound pleasant.

'Could very well be the German nick,' Weir said.

'Where they hang you by your dick,' Oberon concluded.

'And you're dying for a wank,' Dorothy added.

'But the teacher's playing snooker with your balls,' Dorothy, Oberon and Weir, sang in tandem.

'With yoooooour bawllllllllllls,' Weir repeated, going full Pavarotti.

Oberon and Dorothy laughed. Weir chuckled.

'Haven't heard that song in ages,' Weir said.

'An oldie but a goody,' Oberon said.

'Too vulgar for Pacific though,' Weir said with his chuckle.

'Don't play well with others huh?' Oberon asked.

'The strong silent type,' Weir said.

'She only enjoys slit your wrists music,' Dorothy said.

'That true?' Oberon asked.

'That's not true,' I said.

'Sure is,' Dorothy replied.

'Isn't,' I said quickly.

'She has this massive poster on her bedroom wall of a singer who topped himself,' Dorothy said.

'Charming,' Oberon said.

'What about the time we sang *DuckTales*?' I asked.

'*DuckTales,* the kid's cartoon?' Weir said with that chuckle.

'I've always been partial to SuperTed,' Oberon said.

'Teddy Ruxpin all day everyday,' Weir said.

'I don't remember,' Dorothy said.

'You don't?' I asked gently.

'Excuse me all over the place, did I stutter? I just told you, I don't remember,' Dorothy said.

'Now-now keep it classy,' Oberon said.

'Kiss and make up,' Weir suggested.

'I'd pay to see that,' Oberon said.

'You have,' Weir said with a chuckle.

Dorothy watched me wipe smattering of tears from my eyes and she looked angry and then she looked sorry and then she looked out the window.

Weir chuckled as the car came to a juddering stop.

'That's funny,' Weir said.

We were on a deserted road with expansive fields on both sides of us. The trees in the fields were tall and menacing, like they drew their sustenance from eldritch sources. Light was bleeding into the horizon awkwardly, like it was ashamed of itself. Dorothy yawned. Her mouth opened and kept opening. Her face glowed with haughty intensity.

Light moved through the car. I saw it slide across the dashboard which suddenly appeared bulky and oversized. I saw it light up Dorothy's silver bracelet before going through the window to my left. Watching this sweep of light disappear made me want to disappear.

Weir was laughing hysterically. Oberon, having glanced at the fuel gauge, turned to us, said, 'Basically we're out of petrol. Stop laughing, it isn't funny.'

'Pardon?' I asked.

'I wasn't talking to you.'

'You weren't?' I said.

'Weir was supposed to make sure we had enough,' Oberon said, shooting daggers in Weir's general direction.

Weir did not reply. He was too busy laughing, amazed by what his series of chuckles had become.

'So that's that,' Oberon said.

'That-that,' Dorothy said.

'No petrol?' I said.

'Basically none,' Weir admitted between hiccupping guffaws which pitched his body forward so violently I thought he would go hurtling through the windscreen.

'We're trapped,' I said.

'I wouldn't go that far,' Dorothy said.

'How far would you go?' I asked.

Dorothy's mouth, slack from having yawned so much, fell open again. She did not say anything, just gazed at me like I was someone she knew but couldn't quite place. I looked out my window. There was more light in the big wide world making the trees in the fields appear even more menacing, like any second, they would uproot themselves and hurtle towards us, clouds of dust and root balls trailing their wake. Dorothy folded her arms across her chest. The toothpick was missing.

'I saw a petrol station a while back,' Weir said. 'Lucky that,' he added vaguely.

'That's right,' Oberon replied bluntly.

'What is?' Weir asked.

'You seeing a petrol station.'

'Was it wrong I saw one?'

'Not wrong, right.'

'I think I saw a petrol can in the boot, last time I checked,' Weir said.

'How about less with the think and let's stick with the fact you did, shall we?' Oberon said, managing to sound angry and friendly at the same time.

'I'll go get it then shall I? And from there make my jolly way to the petrol station or for shits and giggles, we could all go. Stretch our legs,' Weir suggested.

'You forgot to get petrol so you bleeding well go,' Oberon spat. 'Stretch your bloody legs.'

'Fine, fine, keep your trousers on,' Weir said with a chuckle.

'We'll be here,' Oberon said swivelling his body round and bracing himself with his right hand on the back headrest of Weir's seat so firmly, the leather groaned under the pressure of his fingers.

'Unless Pa-Pa wants to go with. Sorry, I forgot your name,' he said staring at me.

'That's fine,' I said.

'What a fantastic idea,' Dorothy chimed musically. 'You should go with Weir, Pacific.'

'We can ease on down the road,' Weir said with a chuckle.

'That's it,' Oberon said, letting go of the headrest and snapping his fingers, 'Pacific.'

I undid my seatbelt. I opened the door and stepped out the car. My legs felt stiff and standing made me woozy. Weir was by the boot taking out the petrol can. He chuckled before announcing, 'We're off.'

It took a little while getting there.

The proprietor of the petrol station looked up from a glossy catalogue selling bouncing castles when the little bell hooked above the door dinged. Weir paid for the petrol.

It took a little while getting back.

I saw the car. Dorothy was standing in front of it; the purple hibiscus in her hair was gone. Dorothy could not meet my eyes. This was not an issue for Oberon; he was standing next to her, grinning. He was also throwing something in the air and catching it. I saw it shimmer, Dorothy's bracelet. Oberon pretended to throw it like a Frisbee across the field, then did, for real. Weir pulled away from me and pummelled Oberon on his shoulders and when he was done, he offered him a cigarette.

'Smell my finger,' Oberon said.

'Maybe later,' Weir replied with a chuckle

'I want one,' I said.

'Get your own finger,' Weir said.

'Give her one,' Oberon said.

'You don't smoke,' Dorothy said.

I ignored her. I took the cigarette from Weir. He was about to light it for me with his lighter. I told him I wanted to light it myself.

'Whatever the haircut wants,' Weir said, taking a deep bow with all gallantry wrung out of it. He offered me his lighter, with a chuckle.

'No, take mine,' Oberon said. Flaky eczema shadowing his mouth formed a victorious smile a fraction of a second before his lips did. He threw his lighter at me. It bounced off my right shoulder. I picked it off the ground.

'Oops,' Oberon said.

Weir had given me the petrol can to hold when he disappeared into the nearby fields to pee. He whooped, howled, and made a massive spectacle of zipping up his fly while making his way towards me. He doesn't take the petrol can back.

I chucked its contents over the car. No one stopped me. I light my cigarette with Oberon's lighter. I take one slow, deliberate, puff. I throw the cigarette on the car's roof. My aim is perfect. My aim is true. Oberon and Weir stumble back from the car's new, incendiary language. *Whoosh. Wrhhoosh.* Shadows, mine and Dorothy's, twist and contort on the ground. They melt and merge into each other, break apart as I walk away.

Songs 4 Dorothy!   Song Asylum

~~Dorothy's songs~~

Blue field entopic phenomenon

Music for Dorothy.   Good Grief! Dorothy

Over ~~to~~ the Rainbow → July Garland

Hearse of my lonely sleep — Damagod Gods

Cherish the Day — Sade

Tim Buckley — Song ♭ the Siren → Mum's suggestions

Penny's Theme → Inspector Gadget   Dont forget the Back to the Future theme.

~~Elisa in your hand — T'Pau~~

I melt with ~~you~~ with you → Modern English

I Cover the Waterfront — Billie Holiday

This Mortal Coil → Song ♭ the Siren

The Garden is Becoming A Room → Michael Nyman

Love Will Tear us Apart — Joy Division

Subcity → Traci Chapman

High — Noors   Space 4 Rent

Bob Marley and the ~~Whalers~~ Wailers → Redemption Song

Tear in your Hand → Tori Amos

Face ♭ Face → Siouxsie and the Banshees

The Letter → Kristin Hesh

~~Roy Obison → I Drove all Night~~

Colony → Joy Division

Sinnerman → Nina Simone

Slow Fall → The Best Intentions

Ducktales → ? ? ? ? ? ?

More Space 4 Rent